A LONG TIME DEAD

The murder of Napoleon Scotsman the Fourth brought Mark Preston to the mansion called Isobel's Towers. There he met the Towers girls, Angela and Joanna.

The only member of the family missing was Uncle Tommy, who'd wandered off and got himself kidnapped, along with his famous jewellery. Both would be returned for $100,000. Unfortuntely the family couldn't raise it.

Columnist Charles Churchman brought in the Towers Fan Club, and Preston began to wish he'd missed the whole caper. Always excepting the delicious Claire Cilento.

Everything else seemed crazy. Preston didn't realise just how crazy until it was almost too late.

A LONG TIME DEAD

A LONG TIME DEAD

by
Peter Chambers

MAGNA PRINT BOOKS
Long Preston, North Yorkshire,
England.

Chambers, Peter
  A long time dead.

  ISBN 1-85057-526-6

First Published in Great Britain by Robert Hale Ltd, 1981

Copyright © 1981 by Peter Chambers.

Published in Large Print 1988 by arrangement with the copyright holder.

Printed and bound in Great Britain by
Redwood Burn Limited, Trowbridge, Wiltshire.

CHAPTER 1

The murder of Napoleon Scotsman the Fourth did not make the front pages. In fact, it didn't even get tucked away on page seventeen. Outside of the immediate family, the only person in the entire world who knew anything about it was me. At least, in the beginning.

A rusted iron gate stood firmly closed against intruders, and I had to climb out of the car to shift it. The squeaks and groans of the ancient metal offended against the sunlit tranquility of that sheltered valley off the Cahuenja Pass. A few dozing birds peeked down from tree-branches to inspect the intruder, decided I was nobody special, and went back to sleep. I drove along the weed-strewn path leading to the house, curious for my first glimpse of Isobel's Towers. In the days of the great silent movie queens, one of the greatest had been Isobel Towers. She had built the famous house, amid the usual publicity hooha, and being the kind of lady she was, had looked no further than her own name for a house-title. She had been dead for many years, and I knew nothing about the present occupants of the Towers, beyond a name. Drummond. It meant nothing to me, not then.

The place was a disappointment, a cracked and dilapidated version of what must once have been. A great stone Cupid had fallen from his perch and lay neglected along weed-sprouting marble tiles. The pond was a green swamp, and moss grew like a carpet along the lower walls as I approached the front door. There was going to be a butler, naturally. A hawk-faced English type, who would size me up in seconds, and despatch me to the servants entrance. I pressed at the doorbell, and fingered the knot in my tie.

The door opened quickly, and a woman stared out, with a puzzled expression.

"You're not Mr Cornfield," she said snappishly. "Why didn't he come himself? We always have Mr Cornfield personally."

She was fifty years old, trying to look seventy. Graying hair, pulled around into a severe bun, no make-up, and shapeless clothes reaching almost to the ground. Only the eyes, sharp and brilliant behind the vast horn-rims, betrayed the general air of senility.

I smiled encouragingly.

"I don't know any Mr Cornfield, ma'am. The name is Preston. I'm a private investigator. I was asked to come out here to see a Mrs Drummond.

She seemed to stand a little straighter.

"Angie? What do you want with Angie? What's this all about?"

I shrugged.

"I haven't the faintest idea," I assured her. "Perhaps if you let Mrs Drummond know that I'm here——?"

"H'm," she said doubtfully. "Nobody ever tells me anything around here. I'm just part of the furniture, that's what. Well, you'd best come inside, I guess. You can wait there."

She pointed to an ancient hat-rack, where I stood obediently while she bustled away. There wasn't much to look at from my vantage point. A sweeping staircase, leading away from a vast and airless hall, entirely devoid of furniture. From where I was standing, it would be easy to think the place was up for rental, for all the evidence of occupation.

A door opened somewhere to my right, and a girl began to traverse the deserted hallway. Halfway across she paused, turned her head, and saw me.

9

"By the giant jellyfish of Jupiter," she said. "A human being." Walking slowly over, and staring at me intently, she added, "You are a human being, aren't you? Like they show on television?"

I grinned. It wasn't hard to do. My inquisitor was in her middle twenties, with a fresh, open face devoid of make-up. Black hair was piled up thickly on top of her head and kept in place by what looked like a giant meat skewer. I'd thought the horn-rims worn by the first woman were large, but the pair on this tip-tilted nose were coffee-cup size. She wore a one-piece garment, like a painter's smock that had got out of control, and it covered her from her shoulders to an inch short of the floor, where bare brown feet emerged. Shapeless though the smock was, you could tell as she walked that there was nothing shapeless about the contents.

"One human being," I confirmed. "All parts in guaranteed working order. Would you be Mrs Drummond, by any chance?"

She shook her head.

"Not by chance, nor even by design, thank Zeus. Take my advice. Get out of this funny farm before they have you stuffed and stuck in a corner somewhere. What are you doing here, anyway?"

"I'm waiting for Mrs Drummond."

She bit her lip in puzzlement.

"You can't be from the finance company," she mused, "there's nothing left here to repossess. I'm Bill Drummond by the way."

"Bill?"

I said it before I could stop myself.

"Yes. They wanted a boy, you know. Especially my father. Every year I got stuff like boxing gloves and footballs on my birthday. I have a couple of girl's names around someplace, but nobody remembers what they are. I'm just Bill. They still think I'm a boy, sometimes."

"They're wrong," I assured her.

A finger poked at my chest.

"You really think so?"

"No doubt about it."

I hadn't, either. She didn't smell like any boy to me, and if she came much closer in, some form of practical demonstration would be called for. As though sensing the effect she was having, she stepped suddenly back, looking alarmed.

"Oh no, I don't—I don't—" Then she stopped. "Could you lend me a dollar?"

"What for?"

The girl looked around to ensure we weren't being overheard.

"I'm saving up, you see. To run away."

"Run away from what? And I didn't notice any bars on the door."

She pouted.

"Never you mind. How about the dollar?"

"When would I get it back?"

A shrug.

"Probably never, I guess. Oh, Saturn."

Footsteps sounded in the distance. Bill Drummond took off, exiting by the same door as she emerged from. I watched the new arrivals as they marched across the hall. The woman aged fifty going on seventy had been joined by another female, a very different proposition. This one was tall, almost my height, with immaculate iron-gray hair above a commanding brow. The finely-chiselled features carried a combination of beauty and authority, unobscured by the hitherto compulsory horn-rims.

"Mr Preston, good afternoon. I am Angela Drummond."

It was less of an introduction than a state proclamation. It would have been no surprise if half a dozen heralds had appeared on the staircase to blow a fanfare. Not quite shuffling my feet, I said,

"Good afternoon. What can I do for you, Mrs Drummond?"

"Please follow me."

She turned, and proceeded away from me. Not walked. Proceeded. I tagged along behind. The housekeeper, or whatever she was, began to fall into step beside me.

"Not you, Joanna. I'm sure you have plenty to do."

The woman next to me faltered.

"But that's not fair. He was my friend, too."

Angela Drummond turned and paused, fixing the unfortunate Joanna with a look of shafting ice.

"That—will—do."

Joanna crumpled under that withering stare, put a hand to her mouth and said, 'Oh my', and scuttled away.

My prospective employer led me between double doors into what could only be the library.

"Please close the doors, Mr Preston."

They made a heavy banging noise as I pushed them into place. Angela Drummond seated herself on the only respectable chair in sight, and had a good look at me.

"You appear to be well thought of in your particular field, Mr Preston."

It was a promising opener.

"I like to think so," I replied. "Was there

anyone special who recommended me to you?"

She ignored the question entirely.

"One has to be so careful," she went on. "A woman in my position has certain standards, and these must be maintained. The world today is crumbling, Mr Preston, crumbling. Decent behaviour, law and order, ethics, all these things are being forsaken. The evidence is all around us, and things worsen by the day. The old moralities are mocked, the spirit of adventure derided. Today, all we have is the rat race. That is not my expression, you understand, but one I have learned from the popular press."

I made a face to show I understood that such an expression could never have been coined by this formidable woman. She nodded, almost as though I had spoken.

"I see you take the point. The world outside is rushing headlong into disaster. There is nothing I can do to prevent that. But—" and she fixed me with an imperious gaze, "—within these walls, we continue in the old ways. You may think of it as living in the past, if you choose. I prefer to take the view that we here live by principles which are no longer fashionable, but which are none the less right for all that. A bastion, Mr Preston,

14

of an older and greater America. Who knows, if there are enough people of my persuasion, perhaps when the inevitable cataclysm occurs out there, this country may rise again, stronger and better than ever. And so, you see, there must be no chinks in the armour. We must stand foursquare, must be ready and able to withstand criticism. We cannot afford to let the standards slip, for if we do, where can right-thinking people turn?"

I nodded encouragingly. We were getting to it now, I could tell. All this prologue about behaviour and ethics and standards and so forth, this was for openers. Sooner or later we would get to the part about Uncle Willy having robbed his own bank, or whatever.

"It must be extremely difficult to carry on," I contributed, "what with all the responsibility here, and everything."

I flapped a hand around to indicate the general area of responsibility.

Mrs Drummond nodded.

"Exactly. They say virtue brings its own reward, Mr Preston. That may be as it may, and certainly I seek no acclaim merely for living in the way I know to be right. Not everyone agrees with my ways. One makes enemies, naturally. It is a curious reflection on the nature of man, do you not think, that people who live by high principles are seldom popular? That they should frequently be, indeed, the subject of derision, and worse? One grows accustomed to it. The whispering, the scorn. None of it has ever disturbed me in the slightest, all down the years. But now that it comes to murder, I will no longer turn the other cheek, will not tolerate—"

Murder. The word registered with a dull thud, and sank to my stomach like a lead weight. She was still rattling on about her virtues when I said, half-hoping to be contradicted.

"Murder? You did say murder, Mrs Drummond?"

Annoyed at the interruption, she stopped in mid-flow, and looked at me disdainfully.

"Certainly. A shot through the head from a firearm would come into that category, I believe?"

Growing more unhappy by the second, I nodded agreement.

"It would certainly seem so. Who exactly was murdered, Mrs Drummond?"

She clenched and unclenched her hands in rapid succession, and was silent for a moment.

"My dearest and closest friend, Napoleon Scotsman the Fourth."

16

The name meant nothing to me.

"When was this?"

"Sometime last night."

Last night? Then where were the police, the coroner's men, the reporters? Surely this crazy woman didn't think you simply called in a private investigator to tidy up any unpleasantness?

"The police—" I began.

"Police? Bah. Ill-mannered brutes, chewing cigars and shouting at everyone. Prying into every corner of one's private life, and to no purpose. No, I don't think we need trouble the police, thank you."

I looked around for a telephone. If Angela Drummond thought I was going to be an accomplice to covering up the fact of murder, then she had better think again, and fast. Then a thought struck me. If I was going to report a murder, at least I should be certain of my facts.

"Where is the body, Mrs Drummond?"

She let out a long sigh, and waved an arm.

"In the next room."

"May I see it, please?"

"If you must. Come."

She stood up, and walked unwillingly to a single oak door. I tagged along in my usual position. The new room was much smaller

17

than the library, but I wasn't interested in studying the topographical at that moment. A Corgi dog lay stretched out in front of the fireplace, asleep. He didn't bother to look round at the new arrivals. The carpeted floor of the room was otherwise bare. I stared around again to be certain there was no dark corner I could have missed. No corpse.

"Perhaps someone has moved the body, ma'am?" I suggested.

She tutted impatiently.

"Have you no eyes, man? There he lies."

She pointed, and finally I got the message. Napoleon Scotsman the Fourth was a dog.

CHAPTER 2

With comprehension came relief, and a sudden urge to laugh. This I repressed manfully, smoothing away the laugh wrinkles with a hand movement which seemed to indicate deep thought. Well, if this was to be my murder, I'd better get busy on it. Kneeling down, I looked at the dog. There was a single bullet hole in the centre of his forehead, and death must have been instantaneous. The poor little guy certainly hadn't suffered, anyway. He never knew what hit him.

A thought struck me.

"Tell me, does he—or did he used to sleep in this spot?"

She looked down at me, puzzled.

"Quite often. Why do you ask?"

I stood up, smoothing out creases.

"I was just thinking. If he was asleep when this was done, then he wouldn't have felt any pain at all. Thought it might be some comfort for you to know that."

Her features softened for the briefest moment, and she nodded.

"Thank you, Mr Preston. I hadn't thought of that. Well, what are you going to do?"

I was wondering the same thing. This was about to be my first case of dogicide or whatever, and I hadn't much in the way of experience to call on. Looking as profound as I could manage, I said.

"I'm afraid I'm going to have to ask a lot of questions, Mrs Drummond. Could we go back into the library, and perhaps sit down?"

"Very well."

It took a few seconds for us to get settled, and this time I took a chair, a plain wooden affair that must have escaped from some farmhouse kitchen. As a note of formality I took a pad from my pocket, a proceeding noted with approval by my employer. Matters were clearly being put on the right footing.

"The first thing I will ask you is about the weapon," I began. "Is there any kind of gun in the house?"

Her eyebrows elevated one-eighth of an inch.

"Good heavens, yes. Four or five at least. Perhaps more."

The years have taught me never to look surprised.

"Really? Well that's unusual. May I ask why so many?"

She folded her hands together. They were good hands, strong and at the same time shapely, the hands of a more robust artist. Like a sculptress, maybe.

"It started in my mother's time, this security business. She was forever locking things, bolting doors and so forth. My late husband carried on, well, really I suppose I ought to say he was even worse. Burglar alarms, double locks, everything."

"And guns," I supplemented.

"Oh certainly. He always insisted I should carry this special one he bought for me. Silly

20

little thing, I always thought, but it pleased him."

"Where is it now?"

She shrugged.

"I haven't the faintest idea. After poor Augustus died, I put the gun on one side. I've never bothered with it since. It's probably around in the bedroom somewhere. Is it important?"

"Possibly. Tell me about the other guns. Where are they?"

"Let me see, there's usually one in this desk here."

She opened a drawer, found nothing, tried another.

"Yes, here we are."

Her hand appeared above the desk top, and I was staring at the wrong end of a heavy calibre automatic. Nervously, I asked,

"Would you please point that thing away? In fact, put it down altogether."

Obediently she rested it on the leather surface. I got up then and took two strides to the desk. Removing a handkerchief from my pocket, I picked up the automatic and inspected it. There was a light film of dust over the blue metal. I sniffed at the barrel.

"This is a Colt .32," I informed her. "It hasn't been fired recently, so we can rule it out in this case. Perhaps you'd be good enough to put it away again."

It was a relief to see the drawer slide shut. Guns are frightening enough in the hands of people who know how to use them. In the hands of amateurs they are terrifying. At least, to me.

"Well, that's two," I accounted. "Where would we find the others?"

"There's the one over the hall door of course. Great big thing. It couldn't have been used to kill poor Napoleon."

"Why not?"

She sniffed.

"Because it takes great big bullets, huge things. The kind of gun you use to shoot big game."

Deer-rifle then, or bigger. We could rule that out.

"Three," I noted. "Any other handguns that you can recall?"

"Let me see, my husband always kept one in his study. It's probably in there some-where. I'm not sure whether that's the one Bill's always shooting off, or whether that's another one still."

So Bill was the local marksman. Then I remembered I wasn't supposed to have met her. A question would be in order.

"Bill?"

"My daughter," she explained. "She goes off around the garden sometimes, potting away."

With the husband's weapon we seemed to have itemised five guns already, and without really trying. A man could start his own revolution without leaving the house.

"I'd like to see these other weapons as soon as possible," I told her, "but first, perhaps, I ought to ask you who else lives here. And, if you have any day staff, their names too."

She nodded.

"You know about Bill, and you met Joanna, of course."

"Ah yes, the housekeeper."

Her voice cracked across my face like the business end of a bull whip.

"How dare you. Housekeeper indeed. Joanna is my older sister."

I swallowed hastily, grabbing around for excuses.

"Pardon me, Mrs Drummond. I just assumed—that is—"

"Then you assumed very wrongly. The idea."

It didn't seem to cross her mind that if she treated Joanna like the housekeeper, people were liable to get that impression.

"Your sister's surname, if you wouldn't mind."

"The same as my own, naturally. Or rather as my own was. Towers. Joanna Towers. We were the Towers girls, you know."

I haven't known, till that moment, but there were faint stirrings of memory now. Events long gone, and well before my time. But at least I could make one contribution.

"Then your mother was Isobel Towers, the movie star."

She made a small face of disapproval.

"I dislike that expression. So did she. My mother was an actress, Mr Preston, a real one, from the legitimate theatre. The motion pictures may have given her fame and fortune, but they did not create her, the way they did so many of those moronic hat-check girls and worse. Isobel Towers played a whole season with the Barrymores, no less."

Well out of my depth now, I looked around for a floating log.

"That is really fascinating, Mrs Drummond, and perhaps some day we could talk more about it. So, apart from your sister and your daughter, are there any other people in the house?"

She hesitated, put a hand to her throat and stared out the window. For a while I thought

24

she was going to ignore the question, and was about to repeat it, when she said, haltingly.

"It can't possibly be relevant, but there is my aged uncle. Unfortunately, he is not a well man, not well at all. He gets about very little, and never leaves the house under any circumstances."

I looked suitably grave.

"I'm sorry to hear it. Does that mean there's also a nurse here, to tend to his needs?"

"Certainly not," she snapped. "He's not that bad. Or rather, I meant to say, my sister and I are able to look after him quite well, between us."

But the way she had hastened to assure me that he 'wasn't that bad' told me that uncle's problem was likely to be more mental than physical. And Bill Drummond had described the place as a funny farm.

"I'm sure you are," I soothed. "Well, at least this is an all-family household. From my point of view, that is an advantage."

"How so?"

I slid the pad into a side pocket, and looked at her seriously.

"I'm ruling out the possibility that Napoleon was shot by an intruder. You, of course, had already reached that decision before you called my office."

Her eyes narrowed while she digested this. "Had I now? What makes you say so?"

Whatever I said next would have to be said with care.

"Napoleon was shot sometime during the night, you said. That means either by an intruder, or by someone who lives in the house. Why would an intruder want to kill a dog? In the course of a burglary, yes, that I could understand. But there is no burglary here. If there had been, you would have called the police. Or, if, for reasons of your own, you preferred to keep the police out of it, you would have told me. You did not do either of those things. That's point one. Point two is, Napoleon was asleep at the time. Asleep or not, he would have known if there was a stranger around. I don't know much about dogs, but I know Corgis are very smart animals. Napoleon wouldn't just lie there and watch while some stranger was pussyfooting around. This was no stranger. Napoleon had no reason to fear whoever killed him, because he knew that person. You haven't interrupted me once."

Angela Drummond looked faintly surprised.

"Ought I to have?"

"You could have made a protest, tried to argue with me. Because you could see what I was leading up to. I've arrived at the same conclusions you reached many hours ago, Mrs Drummond. Napoleon was killed by one of the family."

She bit her lip, stared at me for a moment, then lowered her head. Her voice was very faint.

"Yes. I know."

Well, at least we'd got that far without any scenes.

"Mrs Drummond, are you sure you want to go on with this? Here we have all your family, all your closest relatives. Wouldn't you prefer to handle it by yourself? Surely a family conference of some kind would be better than having a stranger poking around, causing unpleasantness? Because, make no mistake about it, that's what we're going to have here."

"It would have to be unpleasant, however it was handled."

"That's true. But within the family is one thing. Bringing me in is going to make it worse, not better. If you hire me to dig into this, I will do exactly that. And I won't concern myself about people's wounded feelings and so forth. Not if I want answers.

You'll be hiring me for results, not for my bedside manner."

She sighed then, running a hand along her arm.

"It's almost as though you were trying to talk yourself out of the job," she accused. "Don't you want it?"

"Some of the time I have to trade in misery," I replied, "but it isn't from choice. In it, you understand, not on it. But, you say the word, and I'll get started."

The tall figure rose from the chair, and walked to the window.

"He was my very dear and personal friend," she muttered, almost to herself.

No comment seemed called for, so I sat in silence. Eventually, she turned, and when she spoke again her voice was softer, almost gentle.

"It has been a great comfort to talk to you, Mr Preston. In an all woman household"— the unfortunate uncle clearly did not count— "one comes sometimes to a female-dominated point of view about things. This is not invariably the desirable state of affairs certain of today's leading women would have us believe."

We both managed a faint smile at that one.

"And what have you decided to do, Mrs

Drummond?"

"For the moment, nothing. I was acting out of sheer grief, I can see that now, having listened to what you had to say. I think it would be best if I left the decision overnight, if that's agreeable to you?"

"By all means."

I rose to go. It didn't seem an appropriate moment to mention money, but then, when does it? Before I could say anything, she anticipated me.

"I understand, from my conversation with your secretary, that you charge a three-day minimum fee. That is quite acceptable, of course. So, if I leave it until tomorrow before I ask you to do anything further, I take it that will count as the same three days?"

"Absolutely. In fact, I will go further. I will not accept any other assignment until I have your call."

She inclined her head. If only she wouldn't insist on being so frosty all the time, she'd be a damned good-looking woman.

"Thank you. You are very accommodating. Shall we say by ten o'clock tomorrow morning?"

"That will be fine. I'll wait to hear from you. Please don't bother, I can see myself out."

I left her by the window and opened the huge doors back into the hall. Someone moved at the top of the stairs, and I felt I was being watched as I walked across the hallway to the front door. Before going out, I looked up at the gun Angela Drummond had told me about. She was right about the size of it. One blast from that would have spread the unlucky Napoleon all over the walls. I wondered briefly who had used it, and what had been shot, but it was all a long way from the dead Corgi. Opening the door, I stepped out into the afternoon heat, and walked down broken marble to the car. The trouble with living anywhere near Hollywood is that everybody wants to be an actor, even the cars. Today mine was doing its impression of a steam bath, and I have to admit it does a good job. I opened everything that would open and started the engine.

"Okay Buster, this is a stick-up."

A large black revolver appeared at the side of my head. Behind it was the grinning face of Bill Drummond. Suddenly it didn't feel hot in the car at all. There was quite a chill breeze.

"What's this all about, Miss Drummond?" I asked carefully.

"Just wanted to see what you'd do," she

replied lightly. "Great big tough detective, and everything. Aren't you supposed to grab the gun and beat me over the head with it?"

"Don't tempt me," I begged her. "And for God's sake put that thing down. No, wait. Let me have a look at it."

"Only if you give me a ride in the car."

She made it sound like the request of a twelve year old. I shrugged.

"Won't they miss you?"

"Who, for instance? That bunch in there doesn't even bother to check whether I'm alive, most days."

She walked around the back, and I released the catch on the passenger door. After a moment's hesitation, she shrugged and climbed in beside me.

"The gun, please."

This one was an S. and W., .38, and the barrel reeked of cordite.

"You've been firing this," I commented, trying to sound casual.

"Oh, pshaw," she scoffed. "What a brilliant detective. Tell you something else. If you've got your little box of that powder stuff with you, you'll find my fingerprints on the butt. I always use my fingerprints when I hold things."

I kept hold of the gun.

"Huh," she snorted. Then, "is that true?"

"That's true."

"But I'm the one with the gun. I'm the one who's always shooting at things. On top of that, I'm the oddball in the set-up."

"As to the gun, it's only one of several in the house. Why does it have to be your gun that killed Napoleon?"

"Nobody knows where half the others are. Probably as rusty as hell, anyway."

"Maybe. Let's forget the gun for a moment. Why do you regard yourself as the oddball of the family?"

She tossed her head and the meat skewer wobbled dangerously.

"Pretty obvious isn't it? I'm the only one who's sane."

There was no way I could comment on that without getting into a fruitless argument.

"So now will you tell me what all this planet jargon is about?"

She smiled quickly.

"When I was a child I used to swear like a stevedore. It's got me into all kinds of trouble."

"I can imagine."

As though I hadn't spoken, she went on.

"Nothing seemed to stop me, then Uncle Tommy had this brainwave. He pointed out

34

to me that I wasn't really getting any fun out of it. I only used words that everybody knew, and after a while it was merely boring. Why didn't I work out some cusswords of my own, that nobody could take exception to? That way, I could swear any time I felt like it, and nobody would even realise. It seemed like a good idea, so we worked on it. We came up with the planets. Pretty good, huh?"

"Well, it's a way of dealing with the problem." Then, as a thought struck me, "so what's the equivalent of a Martian sand-blaster?"

She gave a rich chuckle.

"Oh, I never tell. That's the whole fun of it. My gun, please."

"You're not going to shoot me with it?"

"No. I'm quite safe, really."

She held out her hand. Making certain the safety catch was locked on, I passed it over, barrel first. Springing out of the car, she slammed the door.

"Will you be back?"

"I don't know, Bill," I replied truthfully.

"I hope so. It gets lonely out here with all these nuts. Ciao."

There seemed to be a slump to her shoulders as she walked away. I felt sorry for her and annoyed with her, all at the same

35

time. Whatever else she might be, Bill Drummond was not the most restful female I'd ever been around.

On the ride back to town I was thoughtful.

CHAPTER 3

A man of principle should always stand by what he says. The way I saw it, since I'd given Angela Drummond an undertaking that I wouldn't work for anyone else until she passed her time limit, it wouldn't be right for me to go back to the office. There could be all kinds of stuff waiting there, exciting prospects to tempt me away from the narrow path. No, the proper thing for a man of principles was for him to stay away from the action, go home to his own apartment, and stand under a nice cool shower, with a nice cold drink within reach. I proceeded to do those things, and an hour later I was sprawled in front of the tee vee, watching the late afternoon local newscast. Mayor Bloggs assured us that the industrial recession in the area was now well under control, and we could look to the future with confidence.

Senator Cloggs assured us that our views on every issue of importance were being pressed home with vigor in national and even international circles, and we could look to the future with confidence. Coach Hoggs, of the Monkton City Buffaloes, said that a turning point in the team's fortunes had now been reached, mistakes were all behind, and we could look etc. There was a lot of stuff like that, there always is. A man I know claims that our local newscasts are recorded for twelve months ahead, to save the time of busy people, with a one minute spot at the end for notes of anything which is actually happening.

There were slanting shadows in the room now, and I pulled myself reluctantly to my feet, poking around for fresh linen. At sundown in Monkton City, a lot of right-thinking people make for a plush waterhole known as Trail's End. The name sounds more appropriate for an old-time saloon, and that was exactly the way the place began its history long years ago. It had been the place where men had traditionally met to eat, to drink, and in time to arrive at decisions. Elections, lynchings, business deals, all were discussed over foaming beermugs, until in time the place became the recognised institution for most business and civic activities.

There were other, more formal establishments for the conduct of routine in all these matters, but the place where the big decisions were made would always be the Trail's End.

I drove slowly through the thickening early evening traffic, and managed to find a slot at the rear of the premises. There was a man I wanted to see, and at this time of day he would be safely ensconced in his own favourite spot, at the end of the bar in the main lounge. His name is Charles Churchman, though everyone calls him Society Charles. He practically created what passes for society along my stretch of the coast. A New Yorker, he had found the society column business over-subscribed in that great city, and came out to our particular wilderness, as he describes it, almost fifty years ago. There was no shortage of gossip columns and tittle-tattle artists in the trade, but Churchman struck out with a line of his own. He kept away from the smear-business, concentrating on the more acceptable aspects of life and people, especially people. Gradually, he came to be recognised as a source of reliable information, about matters which were worthy of record. He would not attack people, nor attempt to destroy reputations. Many a columnist was read with trepidation by people in high places, but not Church-man. People learned to trust him, to confide in him, and he never disappointed. I was about to give him a few moments of rare pleasure, I had no doubt. Because I had a sudden interest in the Towers family, and that would send him on a journey through his infallible memory-banks, exactly the kind of stuff he thrived on.

There he was, sitting upright in his normal place, as per schedule, with the inevitable glass in front of him.

"Evening Charlie, how're things?"

Very few people are allowed the diminu-tive, and even with those he always hesitates before acknowledging.

، He pursed his lips.

"Ah, the garbage collector. Is it election time already?"

"Coming up, but we don't need to worry. Mayor Bloggs says we can look to the future with confidence."

A delicately-manicured finger pulled at the corner of one eye.

"Really? How reassuring. I wasn't aware that gentleman had any future.

"Oh yes. And Senator Cloggs says—"

"Preston, you've been watching the tee vee news again. It's bad enough that you do such things. You might at least have the common decency not to publicise the fact."

The bartender was hovering near my elbow.

"Beer for me," I told him. "What is that Charlie, a Setting Sun?"

It was a superfluous question. The man has never been known to drink anything else. He watched carefully while his drink was prepared. It's an old habit, from the days when he probably thought a spot of arsenic would be included. Now he leaned slightly forward.

"Preston, you unsettle me. All this largesse, and on top of that you are wearing a clean shirt, obviously for my benefit. Not for nothing, I fear. What is it you want?"

I grinned.

"Met a man the other day who told me he thought your memory was beginning to fail."

"His name, on the instant. I shall sue him for ten million dollars."

I shook my head.

"Couldn't do that to him, Charlie. He has a whole crooked corporation to support. Anyway, I told him he was talking out of his rear end, sorry about that," as he winced, "and here I am to prove him wrong. How are you fixed on Isobel Towers?"

He took the merest sip from his glass,

removed a mauve silk handkerchief from his breast pocket, and went through an elaborate lip-patting procedure.

"My word, you must have been reading the history books. Why the interest?"

Keeping my voice low, I said

"Because I met the Towers girls, quite recently."

I knew from experience that the look on his face was the closest thing he permitted himself to astonishment.

"Can this be true?"

"My word as a cub reporter."

He beckoned suddenly to the bartender, who came quickly.

"What'll it be, Mr Churchman?"

"Is anyone using Mabel?"

"Not right now. There is an eight o'clock booking, I believe."

"We shall be through by then. Please advise the proprietor that Mr Preston and I will be there for the next—say—thirty minutes."

"Consider it done."

For the benefit of anyone who doesn't frequent the Trail's End, maybe I ought to explain what he was talking about. In the old days, the services in the place were all-embracing, if that's the expression I want, and I think it is. There were rooms at the rear, where sympathetic ladies would listen to the problems of the weary traveller on a strictly cash basis. As the town grew, such goings on in a public place could naturally not be tolerated. Amid a great purity purge, with a lot of fanfare and glowing publicity for the leading citizens of the day, the girls were routed out and banned forever from that noble edifice. None of them ever made it to the railroad station, because those leading citizens, with admirable charity and no publicity at all, had thoughtfully made other arrangements. New premises had been provided on the other side of town, twice as lavish, three times as expensive, and strictly members only. But with that coy vulgarity for which my neck of the woods is famous, the names of the evicted ladies were used to denote the vacated rooms. These were now used for business meetings, political chinwags and so forth. It gave schoolkid pleasure to fat and balding executives to be able to say to their secretaries 'If my wife calls, just say I'm over with Mabel', or Lulu, or one of the others.

Mabel would have been astonished to see the way her old room had progressed over the years. Society Charles waved me to a deep armchair and settled himself opposite, after a lot of smoothing and primping. I knew there was no point in trying to hurry the man. Churchman information, when he decided to part with any, was the mother lode. A man had to be prepared to hack at a lot of quartz to reach it. I reached around for my Old Favourites, pushed one into my mouth and lit it. For once, my host didn't bother to register his disapproval.

"Now then," he said imperiously, "the Tower Girls. I have to know every detail, every tiny thing."

"Not much to tell—" I began.

"Permit me to be the judge of that. All of it, please."

"Well, I had this call from a Mrs Drummond—"

I told him the tale, about the house, the people I met there, more or less the whole thing. The part about the dog I kept to myself. It isn't that I don't trust Churchman, but it was the reason my client hired me, and it's no part of my service to go around shouting my clients' business from the house-tops.

"Amazing," he muttered, at the end. "Quite incredible. You haven't mentioned, of course, why it was that Angela Drummond sent for you in the first place."

"No, I haven't."

"H'm. A confidential matter?"

"All my clients' affairs are confidential, unless they tell me otherwise."

His delicate fingers drummed lightly against an elegant leg.

"Do you know, Preston, you've quite cheered me up. The evening was set fair to develop into another crushing bore, like every other evening. Now you come along, with all this lovely chatter about the past. A lesser person than myself might find it almost exhilarating."

Which is as near as he would ever come to admitting excitement. His eyes danced suddenly.

"What would you say if I were to tell you that thirty years ago, the Towers girls couldn't change their shoes without the fact being faithfully reported throughout the world?"

This was what I'd come for.

"I'd say tell me more Charlie. You have both ears."

He pressed his hands together, chin resting on the fingertips, and looked at me impishly.

"Very well, if you want it all, we must begin at the source. With Isobel herself. Did you ever see her—no of course not. Well before your time. Isobel was—in a word—superb. She had grace, charm, beauty, the list is endless. When she came on the screen, you forgot all the other players were there. Projected magic, someone called it. No, it wasn't me, but I'd have been proud to take the credit."

"Her daughter said she came from the legit theatre. Was that true?"

He showed mild irritation at the interruption.

"Certainly. Why do you doubt it?"

"It isn't so much that I doubt it," I told him. "But the Towers lady was a great silent screen star. I even heard of her myself. A lot of those people, men and women alike, didn't survive the talkies because of their terrible voices. That ought not to apply to somebody with stage experience. So what happened?"

Now he twinkled.

"How percipient of you—"

"—percipient, yet—"

"—but you're quite right. Her voice was ideal for the microphone. A mellow fluid sound, that took the public completely by surprise. Just the public, of course, not those who knew her."

'Those who knew her', I was permitted to

infer, included no less a person than Sociey Charles Churchman. He seemed to be needing a prompt.

"So what happened?"

"She made one talking picture, and just before it was released, her husband was killed in an airplane crash. That was his profession, flying. He wasn't anything to do with Hollywood. It was the great tragedy of the year. They were absolutely devoted to each other, and had only just finished building the house. It broke up Isobel altogether. She retired from public life on the spot, and disappeared from view. A few years later, she married again, a much more down-to-earth kind of relationship. The man was a distinguished corporation lawyer. They had two girls, Angela and Joanna."

I thought I spotted a flaw in the story.

"But if Isobel Towers married again, how would her daughters carry her surname?"

Society Charles tutted.

"Really Preston, you must not keep interrupting me. I would have come to that in proper time. However, since you have disturbed the flow, I will tell you. You're not old enough to remember it, but you've probably heard of the Monkton Valley Irrigation Scheme fiasco?"

I dug in the files.

"Some kind of large-scale public swindle wasn't it?"

"Large-scale it was. Gigantic would be more à propos. If they'd pulled it off, it would have been the biggest land-grab operation since the Oklahoma Territory. Fortunately, it was baulked in time, and the principals all received heavy prison sentences. Needless to say, the lawyers involved were the most culpable. One of those was Isobel's husband. They gave him twenty years, but he didn't make it. He died of, I think, pneumonia, after three or four years' incarceration. It finished Isobel, so far as marriage was concerned. She had the girls' names changed legally to her own, and that was the name they grew up with."

He paused for a moment. Not wanting to annoy him with further interruptions, I filled in the gap by grinding out my cigarette in Mabel's ashtray.

"The Towers girls had everything, Isobel saw to that. They were as fine-looking a pair of females as you could wish to see."

I thought back to my encounter with them earlier that day. Well, people change with the years.

"They were attractive, fashion-leaders so

47

far as clothes were concerned. Sportswomen, too. Horse-riding, swimming, tennis, everything. I doubt if there were two sisters on the whole coast more popular. There were plenty of men after them, naturally. Angela married this man Drummond, I recall. He was nobody special, and it was my guess he was after her money as much as the girl herself."

The reference to money must have produced a reaction on my face, because he looked at me sharply.

"I see you're interested in that aspect."

"Well, all I know is what I saw out there today. The place is almost bare of furniture, there aren't any domesic servants, not even for the garden work. The place is dilapidated, Charlie. If there's money around, they must keep it in a tin box under the bed. Not that I'd be very surprised to hear that."

He nodded abstractedly, as though his thoughts were far away.

"Sad. It was all very sad. They hadn't been married very long when Isobel died. She left very little. Must have spent it all in bringing up the girls, I fancy. Anyway, there it was. And, quite shortly after that, the man Drummond left Angela flat. Which seemed to give weight to my theory."

"She told me he was dead," I objected.

Churchman shrugged.

"He may well have died since. It was years ago. Hardly important either way is it? The point is, he left her."

"Joanna didn't marry, then?"

"I think not. No, no I'm positive not. I wouldn't have missed an item like that. She had some illness, I recall, in her early twenties. Dear me, what was it now? It'll come back. But it took her out of the social whirl, that much is certain. Confined her to the house for a very long time. Judging by your experience today, it would seem she never emerged again."

I pulled the pack of Old Favourites from my pocket, caught his expression, and put them back again.

"What about this uncle? Where does he fit in?"

He let me hear his celebrated brittle laugh.

"That must be Tom Towers, I imagine. Isobel's brother, a most engaging rascal. Used to be in vaudeville, you know. Some kind of magic act, I recall. When Isobel made such an impact on the big screen, little brother Tom packed up his box of tricks, and came out to get in on the act. He did quite well, too, as a support comic. Hero's friend, you know the kind of thing. Whereas Isobel was a leading social figure of the most correct kind, Tom was almost as prominent in the bleachers type of society. Caused her a lot of embarrassment more than once, I remember. You say he's a little light-headed these days?"

"I only know what I was told. I didn't actually see him. He'd be getting a bit long in the tooth by now, wouldn't he?"

Even as the words came out, I was trying to claw them back before he heard them.

"It doesn't say anything about tact on your business stationery, does it? Just as well. You couldn't be more wrong Preston. Tom Towers is at the very prime of his life just about now. I believe he's rather more than a year younger than me."

I made the best I could of it.

"It's your own fault, Charlie. You're so active, and you look so young, nobody ever thinks of you as being more than about fifty years old."

Slightly mollified, he sniffed, brushing at his sleeve. Lord knows why. The speck of dust that would dare settle on him hasn't yet been born.

"One tries to keep oneself fit."

We talked for a few minutes more after that. Then I thanked him and got ready to leave.

"Just before you go, dear boy, you wouldn't forget an aged columnist if some little thing were to crop up? Some little tidbit, you know. It would be a rare joy to have some echo of palmier days among all the sludge about these singing drug-addicts."

"If there's a story, Charlie, you get it. Thanks again."

On the way out, I resisted the temptation to leave a little something behind for Mabel.

CHAPTER 4

Next morning I breezed into the office a few minutes after nine o'clock. Florence Digby had her back to the door, delving into a file-cabinet.

"I won't keep you a moment," she called pleasantly.

It was an interesting experience, to see how she treated visitors. I stood there, leaning against the desk and admiring the rear view. La Digby is a lady of indeterminate years, with a figure that would send the average twenty year old screaming for her diet secrets. She is also a neat dresser, always

51

cool, immaculate and conservative. The office is the place for working, not for anatomy displays, and she keeps it that way. On top of all that, she runs the whole place, not excluding the guy whose name appears on the door. I simply provide the raw materials of my enquiries, and she transforms them into reports, expense accounts, correspondence, bank statements, bills in and bills out. You name it, Florence has it covered.

"Sorry to keep you," she turned around, smiling. "I was having—oh. You're very like Mr Preston. Did anyone every tell you that? He usually comes in to the office, but it won't be until much later in the day."

"Nice to see you, too," I assured her. "Expecting a call from yesterday's client. Mrs Angela Drummond, you remember?"

Having recovered her composure, she went behind her desk and sat down.

"Naturally I remember," she advised me tartly. "As a matter of fact, I was talking to the lady just a few moments ago. She seemed rather upset."

So I'd missed her.

"Upset about what? My not being here?"

Florence half-nodded.

"Partly that, yes. But I had a feeling there was more."

The years have taught me to have a certain respect when Florence has a feeling.

"So how's it left? Will she call again?"

"I suggested, with you being so busy and everything"—for 'busy' read 'unpredictable'—"that it would be better if I called back when you were available."

I bowed, and made for my own office.

"Now available. Any mail in there?"

"One insurance bulletin about a missing yacht."

Great. That was one item unlikely to come my way. I read the flier out of nosiness, and the telephone rang.

"I have Mrs Drummond for you," crackled Florence.

"Thank you. Good morning, Mrs Drummond. Sorry I was out when you called. Have you made a decision?"

Her voice sounded almost dreamy, as though her mind was concentrating on something totally different.

"Decision? Ah, well, as to that—" Then she paused. "Mr Preston, there has been a—a development. Yes, a development. Not something about which I really wish to speak with you on the telephone. Would you come out to the house this morning?"

It was unexpected. There's a bar I know

down at the beach. It has a long sweeping verandah facing out to the sea. I'd been half hoping that when the sun got into its stride, I might take up a position on that verandah, and just keep one eye posted seawards, in case a missing yacht should pass. Still, a development is a development.

"I could make it around ten thirty, if that would be convenient."

"Thank you. I shall expect you then."

I kept the receiver to my ear as she replaced her phone. A moment later there was a second click. Somebody else had been listening to the call on a house extension. Then I told myself to stop being such a big detective all the time. If it was going to become a crime for nosey relatives to listen to other people's phone-calls, we'd need a lot more jails.

Still.

At ten twenty five I was outside that iron gate again. But this time, when I heaved it swung smoothly back. Curious. I looked at the hinges. There was fresh black oil on them. Maybe it was time for the annual lubrication job.

There was no welcome committee at the front of the house. I heard the hollow clanging of the bell from somewhere deep inside. Joanna Towers opened the door, and looked at me.

"So you're back."

She made no move to let me in.

"And expected," I assured her. "How are you today, Miss Towers?"

Evidently she was not accustomed to being addressed directly like that.

"Oh dear," she fluttered. "Oh my. Well, yes, I'm very well, thank you, Mr—er— Mr—?"

"Preston" I supplied.

"Yes, Mr Preston. Thank you. Please come in, won't you?"

I stepped inside, and on impulse pointed upwards at the big sporting gun.

"I was looking at that yesterday. A very fine piece. Did it belong to Mr Drummond?"

"Eh? Oh—er—yes. Yes, that is so."

Her eyes were darting about, as if to find some avenue of escape from this business of conversation.

"You must all have missed him very much," I condoled, "a sad loss, I'm sure."

Now she fixed her eyes on me sharply.

"Sad loss? What sad loss? What are you talking about, young man?"

"Why, Mr Drummond, of course."

Joanna became agitated, and bony fingers

scrabbled at my arm.

"Augustus," she exclaimed. "Something's happened to Augustus? What've you heard? Tell me now."

I put on a puzzled expression. It wasn't all put on.

"Why, nothing" I assured her. "I haven't heard a thing about Mr Drummond. Only what Mrs Drummond told me."

"Told you? Told you what? What did she tell you?"

I removed her sharp hand gently.

"Only about her husband being dead."

"Ah. She told you that?"

"Why, yes."

"H'm."

She gave a snort, took a pace back, and inspected me, with her head tilted to one side.

"Angie told you he was dead, huh? She would. She just would."

There was a change taking place in her as she stood there. Her back was getting straighter and her shoulders were pulling back. As this happened, the years were falling away. Nobody would mistake the woman now standing before me for an old lady. Facially too, she was tightening up, and I could see more than a passing resemblance to her sister. Something had evidently upset her, to judge by the way she was breathing, and the rise and fall of her bosom.

"Dead? She said that? That's Angie for you. Always was. Absolutely typical Angie."

I held up a hand in an effort to calm her down.

"I'm sorry Miss Towers, but I really have no idea what you're talking about. If I've upset you—"

"You? Nothing to do with you. It's her. It's always her. My loving sister, telling you a terrible lie about poor Augustus. Well, I'll tell you something. Something that is true. Augustus did not die. Not. He ran off and left her, that's what. Just left her. She couldn't stand that. That was one thing she never could stand. No one went off and left the gorgeous Angela Drummond. She wouldn't permit it, you see. So she invented this yarn about him dying. Because that's what it is, a yarn, Mr Preston."

I looked as uncomfortable as I felt.

"Believe me, I'm very sorry to have been the cause—"

"Told you before. Not your fault. Anyway," and she began to slump again, "what does it matter? What does any of it matter now? It's all so long ago. So many years. It doesn't matter, you see?"

As she spoke her posture had been crumpling, and I was once again looking at the little old lady I'd seen on my first visit. The whole transformation had been a remarkable business. Spooky, to say the least. It would be safer in future to avoid any attempt at conversation with this one.

"Where will I find Mrs Drummond, please?"

"In the library."

She pointed vaguely, and turned to go. Then she changed her mind, and looked at me again, her face almost kindly.

"Would you like some coffee?"

It was on the tip of my tongue to refuse, then I changed my mind.

"That would be very nice, thank you."

Nodding, she shuffled away. I shook my head and made for the great double doors.

"Ah Mr Preston. You are on time. Good."

She was back in the good chair again, waving me towards the kitchen variety. I sat down, inspecting her.

The trouser suit was gold lame, and her hair had been swept up, à la Grecian. The eyes and face had been lightly but expertly made up. This Angela Drummond was ten years younger than the one I'd spoken with

58

the day before. Isobel Towers had left both her daughters more than her name. If anything, her outward appearance was even more composed than before, and yet there was something. It wasn't in the eyes, they were direct enough, perhaps there was an indefinable air about her. I couldn't pin it down exactly, but there was something about her that was not quite at ease.

"Some refreshment, Mr Preston? A drink perhaps?"

I tried not to shuffle my feet.

"Well, as a matter of fact, your sister was kind enough to offer me coffee. I'm afraid I accepted."

There was just a hint of frost in her tone when she said,

"Really. How thoughtful of her. My sister is not usually so forthcoming. You must have made a good impression. I thought I heard voices in the hall. What did you find to talk about?"

"Nothing. Just generalities, you know. I asked her about your late husband's rifle. The one that hangs over the door."

"What about it?"

"Nothing about it. Like I say, I was just making conversation."

"Ah."

She seemed satisfied at that. I was relieved. It was no ambition of mine to go stirring up a fight between these two. Joanna herself saved the moment by appearing with a loaded tray. Advancing into the room, she announced in tones of near-defiance.

"Mr Preston said he would like some coffee."

"Thank you, Joanna. What a good idea. I would have asked you to stay and join us, but I know you have a million things to do."

I looked at the tray, with its three cups. It would seem that Joanna had arrived all prepared to let the million things wait a while, but her sister's words put paid to any such idea.

"Yes. Oh yes, I really must get on, if you'll excuse me."

She bustled out again, while Angela watched with a set face. What was it, I wondered, what history of circumstances had created this mistress and servant relationship between the two girls? Because they must have been only girls or young women when it started. The situation I was observing had not been created in a few months.

Angela fussed around with the coffee pot, and I went over to collect the steaming cup. When I was settled again, I thought it was

60

time to get down to business.

"You said on the telephone that there had been some kind of development."

She made a slight moue.

"You are very direct."

Well, what did she expect? Maybe I should have spent twenty minutes asking after the geraniums.

"Sorry. In your own time, naturally."

She dipped the Greek hairstyle at me.

"First, I want to explain to you about Uncle Tommy."

I resisted an impulse to tell her what I already knew about him. It would be more polite to let her talk. It might also be more revealing, because if she jazzed up the disappearance of her own husband, maybe she would cast Uncle Tommy as a retired Southern senator, or better.

"Ah yes, your indisposed relative," I said, looking grave.

She sipped at her coffee, and set down the cup.

"Uncle Tommy is my mother's brother, her younger brother. He followed her into the theatre, and was just beginning to achieve success as an actor when Isobel came to Hollywood in such triumph. Once she was established, she sent for him to come and join

61

her, which he did. Unfortunately, he did not meet with the same success, and this was true of his social life, as well as his acting career."

She paused, to be certain I was paying attention. I was. I was also comparing her version with what I'd heard from Society Charles Churchman. Apart from omitting the dreaded word 'vaudeville', she was doing all right so far.

"In those days, Hollywood was trying to find its feet, socially. There had been a great deal of unfavourable publicity, and more than one famous trial, concerning the after hours habits of some sections of the community. This brought a twofold reaction from the people of the day. There were responsible people, of whom Isobel was one, who were determined to live by certain standards, to set an example. There were also, regrettably, people who took a different view, and carried on in the most deplorable fashion." She lowered her voice. "I am sorry to say that Uncle Tommy allowed himself to be swept along by those people. His activities were a source of continual embarrassment to the family. He was a womaniser of the worst kind, a heavy drinker, and a man who would gamble a whole month's salary on a one horse race."

Once again she stopped and looked over at me.

"It must have made life very difficult for your mother," I contributed lamely.

"You take my point very well. My mother's first marriage ended in tragedy. The poor man was killed in an airplane accident of some kind. My mother retired from the screen. At just about the same time, Uncle Tommy became involved in a scandal of such magnitude that no studio would ever hire him again. Mother took him in, of course, and they remained together until the end. Until she died, that is. By then he was so much one of the family that it never occurred to anyone to ask him to leave."

"I see. So this scandal, whatever it was, quietened him down, I imagine."

"Huh."

It was a most unladylike snort.

"Did you say 'quieten him down'? Well, I'm afraid that is not a correct assumption. He was the bane of mother's existence for years. Oh, he did become much quieter eventually. But that was due to anno domini, not any change in his nature."

Whether it was just my natural perversity, or an automatic kinship with a fellow-male I don't know, but I found myself warming to

63

the horrendous Uncle Tommy.

"These days, he is extremely well-behaved, mainly due to lack of funds. In addition, he is no longer quite as reliable in the mind as he once was. He tends to forget things, and is quite unsafe in traffic or in crowded places. Do not misunderstand me, Mr Preston, my uncle is not unbalanced. But he does need care. Care and constant surveillance."

"I think I have the picture, Mrs Drummond. Forgive me, but why are you taking all this trouble to tell me about your uncle?"

Angela Drummond sighed, and clasped her hands together on her elegant knees.

"Because Uncle Tommy has wandered off. Sometime between dinner last evening and breakfast. And that isn't all."

It was as though she was reluctant to finish the story.

"I'll have to have it all, you know," I prompted, as softly as I could.

"Yes, yes of course. When we'd all searched high and low, I began to wonder about poor Napoleon again. You see, I had thought—well, never mind what I had thought. Suffice it to say that Uncle Tommy's disappearance set me off thinking. You will recall that I told you about the various

64

guns we have in the house? Well, two of them are missing. The little one from my bedroom, and the one from my late husband's desk."

"Two?" I echoed. "Needless to say, you've searched thoroughly?"

"The house has been turned upside down, Mr Preston. There is no sign of either of them."

This was a development I didn't like. If she'd said one gun, I'd have been tempted to write it down as carelessness, and expect the weapon to turn up in some unexpected corner, sooner or later. But two guns put a different complexion on things. It also put me in a difficult position.

"Before I ask you to go on, Mrs Drummond, I should warn you that we have a potential police situation here."

She raised her finely etched eyebrows.

"Police? Oh, you mean the Missing Persons people. I'm hoping that will not be necessary."

I shook my head.

"No. I mean the missing weapons people. It is a condition of your firearms permit—I am assuming you have one, by the way?—"

"—certainly, yes—"

My relief was not assumed.

"Very well. It is a condition that the

65

safekeeping of the weapon is the responsibility of the license holder, and that if the weapon is lost or stolen, the matter must be reported."

"Oh. I was not aware of that. Mr Preston, please, I most certainly do not wish the police to be involved here. I thought I made that plain yesterday."

"Yes, you did. But yesterday we did not have this felony situation. That's what it is, if a missing weapon is not notified. However, we needn't concern ourselves with that immediately. You can always say you are still searching. For a while, at least. Tell me, and I realise this must be painful for you, are you now saying that you think your uncle shot Napoleon, and has run off with the gun?"

She heaved the splendid shoulders.

"What else am I to think, Mr Preston? You are going to find him for me, aren't you? Before he gets into any trouble, or someone out there hurts him?"

There was a little-girl element in the appeal. The big strong detective will go and make everything better. I didn't want to tell her the statistics on Missing Persons in our sunlit state.

"You have no idea where he might have gone? No old friends for instance?"

"None."

It sounded hopeless from where I sat. But I knew I'd have to make a token showing.

"Then I must ask you a lot of questions, I'm afraid. First of all, let me have his description. Let's start with his height."

It took the greater part of an hour. One factor was particularly interesting. She told me he'd taken all his jewellery.

"Jewellery? But I thought he was a poor man?"

"Oh, he is. It isn't real any more. But it was once, all of it. He used to walk around wearing a fortune. Stick pin, cufflinks, rings on his fingers, all top grade gems. All imitation now, of course. I mention that he's taken those things only to illustrate the seriousness of his absence. He would never travel far without his baubles."

Shortly after that, I rose to go.

"Would there be any point in my talking to the others? I mean your sister or your daughter?"

"I'm sure not. They are just as fond of him as I am. If either of them had the remotest idea where to look, they would have suggested it to me at once."

"Very well. I'll get back and start making some enquiries."

She rose from her chair, holding out her hand. It was firm and dry.

"I'm not a wealthy woman, Mr Preston, but I am prepared to spend a great deal of money to find that foolish old man."

I pressed her fingers warmly.

"Who knows? I might get lucky at the first stop. Oh, by the way, what are you doing about Napoleon?" I nodded towards the oak door. "Is he still in there?"

"Heavens, no. Mr Cornfield came and saw to things, thank you. It's all been taken care of."

Cornfield. That was the name Joanna had used when she answered the door to me the day before.

I went back to the car, half-hoping that Bill Drummond would show up, preferably without her popgun.

But there was no one, and I drove slowly away.

CHAPTER 5

All I had to do was list all the places I'd be likely to find a well-dressed septuagenarian, who may or may not be slightly off-centre in the brain department, and who would be packing two guns. Where would such a man go? By the time I got back to the office I still hadn't a single idea in my head.

Florence had gone out to lunch, so I had the place to myself. I poked around on her desk to see if there were any messages, but there was nothing. Sitting behind my own shining leather top, I racked my brains for some kind of inspiration. Uncle Tommy's picture lay in front of me. It was ten years old at least, but Angela Drummond had assured me he'd hardly changed at all. He was a tall, spare-looking man, with a shock of white hair, and a look on his face that told me at least some of the tales about the women and the gambling were true. He didn't get to look that way teaching Sunday school.

There was a noise in the outer office. My watch said the Digby was back from lunch

69

early.

"I'm in here, Florence," I called, then got back to my musing.

A voice said

"Don't call me Florence, it's bad for my image."

I looked up then, to see a man standing in the doorway. He was tall and broad, with a clean-shaven face he'd been using about thirty years. The no-crumple lightweight suit must have rung in at four hundred dollars minimum, and all his other accoutrements shouted money. Some people leave their jackets unbuttoned because they're too fat, or on account of the heat. With others it's because they can reach inside fast if there's anything under there they might need in a hurry.

"So you're not Florence," I conceded. "Who are you, and what do you want?"

He nodded pleasantly and took another step inside.

"Come to talk a little business. It's kind of delicate."

"Most of my business is," I retorted. "Anyway, I'm tied up right now. Could it wait a couple of days, Mr—?"

He ignored the question, and came closer still.

70

"This can't wait. Kind of urgent, you understand. An old man sent me. He's in a little trouble, and your name came up."

Old man. My spine tensed for a moment.

"There are lots of old men," I hedged. "Does he have a name?"

He was directly across the desk now.

"Do you have any artillery around?" he demanded.

"Why do you ask?"

"Just nosey, I guess. I'll show you my gun if you'll tell me where yours is. Look."

The unbuttoned coat moved smoothly aside. The butt of a black automatic protruded from his waistband. He grinned.

"Your turn."

"In the desk drawer."

"Let's take a look."

I hesitated. If I was very quick, I might get the .38 out of the drawer in time to blast the visitor before he could draw his own weapon. The odds were about even. But what would be the point? He hadn't come here to shoot me out of hand. He could have done that anytime in the last two minutes. No. What he wanted was talk, with him holding the upper hand, if needed.

Shrugging, I slid open the drawer. He leaned over and peeked inside.

71

"Key?" he queried.

The key was on the same ring as my car keys. I showed him. He nodded.

"Fine. Just lock it away, huh? So we can all be comfortable?"

I turned the key in the lock, and he held out his hand for the bunch. When I handed them over, he grunted, and laid them on the far corner of the desk, out of quick reach.

"Who's Florence? Lady friend?"

"My secretary. She's due back from lunch anytime."

One long leg reached out behind him, and he kicked the door shut. Then he sat down on a facing chair.

"O.K. We talk."

"Let's talk about the old man," I suggested. "Who is he?"

Although I already had a nasty feeling about that.

"Name of Towers. He's Mr Thomas Towers. Mean anything?"

"It might. But I've never met him, and that's the truth. And yet you say he sent you here. There has to be more."

"Oh there is, there is. The old guy walked into a hockshop this morning, bold as brass. Said he wanted to hock a stick pin, with a big diamond on the end. The jeweller took one look at it, and knew it was class merchandise. Too much class, for a little man like him. He knew he was looking at twenty thousand dollars, or better. In fact, when we got a second opinion, the figure turns out to be nearer forty grand. Imagine."

It made no sense. Angela Drummond had told me that her uncle's stuff was all trash.

"I still don't see where I come in. So he hocked a jewel. So what?"

"Ah. There's more."

I'd known there would be.

"You see, this old gent was covered in stones. On his strapwatch, cufflinks, all over the place.. If the stickpin was worth so much, how much was he toting around altogether? The guy in the hockshop made a phone-call. To some friends of mine. They said to stall the old man till they got there. Now they have the old man, they have all his stuff, and they want to trade?"

Great. Uncle Tommy had walked into a den of thieves. Now I had a kidnap on my hands.

"This makes no sense," I grumbled. "I know all about Mr Towers, and the way he dresses up. That stuff is all glass. I doubt whether you'd clear five hundred bucks on the whole collection."

73

"Uh huh."

My visitor reached in a side pocket and pulled out a matchbox. Sliding it open, he tipped it over. A hundred coloured lights flashed in the sunlight on the desktop, as a small gem rolled to a halt.

"Sample. Take a look at it."

Gingerly, I picked it up and rested it in the palm of my hand. I don't know anything about precious stones, and this could be just glass for all I knew. But the way the entire colour spectrum danced from every facet told me otherwise.

"I'm no jeweller," I stalled.

"Me neither. Take it to somebody who is. They'll tell you."

I began to get a feeling, one that I didn't care for.

"You mean I can keep this?"

"Why not? Like I said, it's just a sample. Our man says that little item registers about fifteen hundred dollars. Have it checked. There are eleven others like it on the watch alone."

I placed the stone carefully back on the desk. My head was in a whirl, trying to reconcile what this character was telling me with the story I'd had from Angela Drummond.

74

"Look, I'm getting out of my depth here,"
I confessed. "The old man is supposed to be a
broker, and yet you come in here telling me
he's worth a lot of money. How much money
by the way?"

He pursed his lips.

"It shakes down at half a million. Give or
take a few cents."

Wow. If that were true—no, I didn't
believe it. Yes, I did believe it. I didn't want
to believe it. Even if it were true.

"So what happens now?"

The answer to that was plain enough, but I
just wanted to keep the guy talking as long as
possible. That way, my own confused mind
could just begin to come up with something.
At the moment, everything was a blur.

My visitor had a pleasant smile.

"Now, we talk. Some friends of mine,
they've done this kind of work before. Stones
like these are insured and listed. Could take a
long time to get them unloaded. We wind up
with a third of the price, and there's always
just a chance somebody gets himself caught.
We like the cash and carry business. What
they call a quick turnover. The insurance
company ought to go for ten per cent. Saves
trouble all round."

"Ten per cent of half a million would be,

let's see—"

"Fifty thousand."

That was what I'd feared.

"So I go to the company and put the bite on them. Then what?"

He heaved his shoulders.

"What do you want, diagrams? Then we trade. We get the money, you get the stuff."

I wagged a finger.

"You left out the part about letting Mr Towers go."

"One thing at a time. Now we talk about the old guy. He's a nice old guy, you know? The loving family ought to shell out a few bucks of their own. Say another fifty Gs."

This was bad news. The part about the insurance company was at least a viable proposition, something to work at. The prospect of Mrs Drummond being able to lay hands on that kind of money was a different matter entirely. From what I'd seen of the state of the house, the lack of furnishings, and so forth, I didn't think there was even an outside chance she could raise that kind of money. I tried to explain to him.

"Look, the insurance part, maybe we have something there. At least I can try. But as to the family, there's no money there. Listen, I've met the people, been to the house. I don't think there's any way they could scratch up five thousand, let alone fifty."

Disbelief was written on his face.

"You expect me to fall for that? Here's this man, walking around the streets like a diamond mine on legs, good clothes. Kind of old-fashioned, mind you, but good clothes. And here's you trying to tell me the family is on relief. Quit stalling around."

Trouble was, I could see how it must look, from his angle.

"I can't explain the jewellery," I admitted. "Even his own niece thinks it's glass. As to the rest, Mr Towers is all front. It comes natural to him. He used to be a movie actor, you know."

"Who didn't?" shrugged the other. "Every other person you meet around here, if they're over sixty years old, they'll tell you they used to be movie stars. This hogwash ain't gonna work, Preston. You just get in touch with the loving family, and see how fast they shell out."

"And if they can't?"

When he spoke, the tones were very flat.

"If they won't pay, then we'll know they don't want him back."

I wasn't going to make any impression on this man by further argument. There was another angle, one that hadn't come up so far.

"All I can do is tell them what you say," I replied quietly. "But let's get back to the jewellery. You're assuming the stuff has to be insured. The family thinks it worthless. That being so, I doubt whether there is any cover. What happens if I'm right?"

He shook his head again. It was clear he was finding it very hard to believe anything I said. I really couldn't blame him.

"All right, you wanna play games, Preston, let's play. If everybody says there's no insurance, that means no list. Without a list, the goods are practically impossible to trace. To us, that's only good news. We can go trading. Instead of ten per cent, we could wind up with fifty. A quarter million dollars. So you see, we only gain here, whichever way it floats."

"And the old man?"

"Same deal. We can buy a lot of concrete with a quarter million dollars."

He said it so matter-of-factly that I knew there was no room for discussion. There was still one thing that puzzled me.

"Let me tell you something," I began. "I'm doing a little work for Mr Towers' niece. Until yesterday, I never laid eyes on her. I've still never seen Mr Towers, like I told you. I don't understand why you came to see me with all this stuff. Why didn't you go straight to the family?"

He listened carefully, then nodded.

"Yeah, well we talked about that, you know? According to our pal, the movie star, there's nothing but women in the family. Not much of a bunch, either, the way he tells it. The top lady sounds like some kind of nut, herself. We like to deal with a man. Dames are nowhere in this kind of business. First they shout for the smelling salts, then they start raising posses. Everybody gets to chasing his own ass, and nothing gets done. They don't stop to think. Now, a man, he chews things over. Take you. You know just what's going to happen if anybody blows any whistles. Right?"

I knew the answer to that.

"That's the last anybody sees of you, or the jewels, or Uncle Tommy."

"You got it. Say, is that what they call him, Uncle Tommy? That is nice. Suits the old guy. I'll call him that. Make him feel kind of like at home, you know?"

"I can see you have good family feelings," I told him nastily.

He shrugged.

"Yeah, well, this is business, you know?"

"Supposing, and I'm only supposing, we can get together on the money angle. What's to stop you from killing the old man anyway? It's been done before, and there's always the chance he could identify you."

He listened attentively, then nodded agreement.

"Check. I can understand where you would think that way. Like you say, it don't make sense to turn a good kidnap witness loose on the streets."

"Well, then—"

"Don't interrupt me. I said a good witness. You never met dear old Uncle Tommy, you said so yourself. Well, I'm here to tell you that man would be no kind of witness to anything. Most of the time he's O.K., but then his mind kind of wanders away, you know? A kid doing his first year law school could make mincemeat out of Uncle Tommy the minute he got on the stand. Take my word, don't worry about that angle. We'll send the old coot home in one piece. We don't want to hurt him. But, we must have the dough first."

He stood up suddenly.

"That cuts it, I guess."

"How do I get in touch with you?" I

queried.

His teeth were very clean.

"Stop kidding around. I'll call you."

"This is going to take a little time—" I hedged.

"Keep it that way. A little time is all you have. I'll call you tomorrow."

There was one final point sticking in my mind.

"Before you go, there's another thing. You say Uncle Tommy would make a lousy witness, and I guess it's true. But there's one other man, he'd make a very good witness indeed. I'm talking about me. When this is over, what happens to me?"

He rested great hands on the desk.

"I'm glad you asked me that. That's the reason they sent me on this deal, to talk to you. I'm just on the coast on vacation. I don't belong around here at all. The local law has nothing on me. You can search for me till you're blue in the face, I'll be gone home. And the other guys, well you'll never see them. So, don't worry about it. You'll be able to sleep nights."

"Do you have a name?"

At the doorway, he paused.

"Call me Mr Small. On account of my size. I'll be in touch."

He went out then. I reached over to retrieve my keys, and unlocked the drawer of my desk. Something told that the drawer was no place for the .38 for the next few days.

CHAPTER 6

When I called Isobel's Towers, the phone was picked up at the third ring. Angela Drummond's voice said,

"Hallo?"

"Mrs Drummond?"

"Yes. Who is this?"

"Preston. I have to see you right away. Shall I come out to the house now?"

Pause.

"Do you mean you've found Uncle Tommy already?"

If her tone was anything to judge by, an affirmative reply would not induce a fit of ecstasy.

"No, not exactly. But I think I may have some information about him."

She didn't quite say tut-tut.

"Well, why don't you tell me what it is?"

I looked to the ceiling for support.

"I'm afraid I can't do that. This is not something that can be dealt with over the phone."

When she spoke again, there was a touch of asperity in her voice.

"You're being very mysterious. Is this cloak and dagger business really necessary?"

"I'm afraid so. And it is urgent."

"Very well, if you insist. But not out here. As it happens, I'm coming into the city quite shortly. I could see you at—let's see—three o'clock?"

"Fine. And one other thing. Will you please bring with you any insurance policy or documentation you may have about Mr Towers' jewellery."

Another pause, while she thought about this new development.

"His jewellery? That assortment of glass? There's nothing like that here, I do assure you. What do you want it for?"

I sighed.

"Mrs Drummond, believe me, I wouldn't ask if it wasn't important. Are you absolutely certain there's nothing?"

"Positive," she asserted. "In any case, I don't keep any papers of that kind out at the house. In case of fire, you know, or burglary. Anything official is lodged with my accountant, Mr Hawke. Of Hawke and Jepstow, that is."

Evidently there could be no question of fire or burglary involving an operation with a name like Hawke and Jepstow.

"How would it be if I telephone Mr Hawke?"

"Out of the question," she snapped. "He would never dream of discussing my private affairs with a stranger."

"That's fair enough. If you're coming into town anyway, perhaps we could both call on him. Believe me, when you hear what I have to tell you, you'll be as anxious about the details as I am. More so, in fact."

"If you insist," she said wearily. "I'll call his office right away. Shall we have our meeting at Mr Hawke's office at three o'clock?"

"No," I rejected the suggestion promptly. "I must speak with you alone, before we see anyone at all. Would you please come here at three, and we'll go along to Mr Hawke together afterwards? Better tell him four o'clock."

"I assure you such a visit will be a complete waste of time."

I hoped my sigh didn't travel down the phone.

"In which case I shall be happy to apologise."

"Very well. I will be there at three."

And she broke the connection. Two seconds later there was a second click. I rubbed my chin, thinking. Putting myself in Angela Drummond's place, and trying to be objective, I really couldn't blame her for taking the attitude she had. It was clear from the way she spoke that she thought I was being over-dramatic and secretive in refusing to discuss my new information. What she had no way of knowing was that I was now actively engaged in withholding information from the authorities on one or two minor infractions of the law. Kidnap, threatened murder, extortion, grand theft, illegal recovery of stolen property, the list was endless. As matters stood, I'd be lucky to get off with nine hundred and ninety nine years if some of the boys down at headquarters got wind of what I was doing.

I picked up the stone Mr Small had left behind. There was time for me to get an expert opinion on that, and grab a bite to eat, and still be back in good time for my appointment with Mrs Drummond.

The phone jangled.

"Preston Investigations," I growled.

Where was Florence Digby? She picked a fine day to get back late from lunch.

"Is that Mr Preston? Mr Mark Preston?"

A man's voice, high-pitched and worried.

"Speaking. Who is this?"

"I am Mr Cooper, of Cooper's Guns and Rifles, Twelfth Street."

I'd been past the place, and had a mental picture of the storefront.

"What can I do for you, Mr Cooper?"

"Are you acquainted with a Miss Drummond?"

The only one I knew was Bill.

"I know a Miss Drummond," I agreed cautiously. "What about her?"

"There is a young lady in the store at the moment by that name. She came in here to sell me a weapon, and she appears to have no proof of ownership. She also has no license for the gun, and of course I cannot conduct business under such circumstances. In fact, I had it in mind to call the police, but she assures me that you will speak for her."

"Could you describe the lady, Mr Cooper?"

He began a vague and rambling description that could have fitted anyone from Minnie Mouse to the Mona Lisa. But when he got as far as the hairstyle, I knew we were in business.

"That sounds like my Miss Drummond," I admitted. "Tell you what, Mr Cooper, I was just about to leave my office anyway. I'd be glad to call in at the store, say, about ten minutes, if that would help?"

He was highly relieved.

"I should be more than grateful. With things the way they are today, we can't be too careful about the movement of these hand-weapons."

"I agree entirely. See you in ten minutes."

As I walked out into the corridor, I met Florence homing in.

"Don't hurry yourself," I said huffily. "I've dealt with all the visitors myself, and taken care of the calls in."

She smiled frostily.

"How fortunate that you should have been in the office, Mr Preston. I have just completed our quarterly reconciliation with the bank manager. He could only fit me in at this particular time, and so I have not been able to take lunch. I trust you will have no objection to my eating a sandwich at the desk?"

You'd think a man would learn not to try getting the better of La Digby. I grinned apologetically.

"Sorry Florence, I guess I'm on edge. Our

client, Mrs Drummond, is due here for three o'clock. I ought to be back by then, but hold on to her if I'm late will you? It's very important."

She inclined her head regally, and swept past me. I was still smarting when I turned into Twelfth Street and located Cooper's. Inside the store, a fat man was having a whale of a time trying to choose an old Western Colt. He probably had a silver mounted gunbelt at home, and fancied himself cleaning up the West. He'd have been better occupied cleaning up that waistline.

A very bald man in a rusty black suit came towards me, with a look of enquiry on his face.

"Mr Preston? I am Mr Cooper. Won't you please come in."

We probably shook hands, but it was such a lightning movement that I couldn't be absolutely certain. In the office, parked on a narrow chair and looking very unhappy, was Bill Drummond.

"Mark, thank God you're here. Will you please tell this—this—store proprietor that I'm not some bank-robber's girl-friend?"

She got no sympathy from me. And she could still be in trouble if Mr Cooper wasn't calmed down. The trouble wouldn't come to anything in the end, but it would involve police, and policemen ask questions. The very last people any of us wanted around Isobel's Towers at that moment were policemen with questions. I had to get alongside Cooper, and fast.

"Keep a civil tongue in your head," I suggested, "you ought to be grateful that Mr Cooper agreed to call me, instead of just marching you down to the precinct house."

"It's only because she has an honest face," chimed Cooper.

"Lucky you take that attitude, Mr Cooper. The family would be struck with horror if they thought there was anything unlawful going on. I can assure you there is no problem about licenses. Miss Drummond's mother takes care of all that side of things. There are several guns about the house, well you know the way it is in these big Valley properties. Sporting guns and so forth. I think I can understand what happened here. It probably never occurred to Bill—that is to say Miss Drummond—that any of the guns belonged to anyone in particular. Is that right, Bill?"

I stared at her hard, willing her to agree with me. She nodded, and contrived a half-smile.

"Well, you're absolutely right, naturally. I mean, it just never occurred to me that—"

"Exactly," I cut in, before she could foul it up. "I suppose it was your usual problem? Your allowance ran out too early again?"

She was catching them well now.

"That old allowance. It might have been enough when grandma was a girl—"

"There you are, Mr Cooper," I turned to him. "I know it's all very foolish and so forth, but you can see the way it is."

He had been buying the act from the beginning. He liked me laying into her that way, and he liked the part about the big house in the Valley.

"Yes, I can see very well, Mr Preston," he agreed. "I have daughters of my own, and their allowances are hopelessly inadequate, if they are to be believed."

We were all men together. At least, two of us were.

"Could I see the gun?"

"Oh, certainly." He opened a drawer and put his hand inside. "A very choice piece indeed. English. A Webley .36. One doesn't see too many of them."

He held it out for inspection. Until that moment, I'd been hoping against hope it was going to be the one Bill had been waving at me

90

when she went into her Bonnie Parker act the previous day. But this gun was new to me.

"Ah yes," I nodded, as if we were old friends. "Let me see, this is the one normally kept in your father's desk, isn't it?"

The girl inclined her head. My mind was beginning to churn again. I took the weapon from Mr Cooper's outstretched hand.

"Once again, let me thank you for keeping this confidential," I said gravely. "I think Miss Drummond and I had better be on our way."

I poked the Webley into a side pocket. The gunsmith watched.

"As I say, a very choice piece. I could give a very favourable price," he said tentatively.

"Thank you, I'm sure it's well known that a man always gets an honest deal from Cooper's. However, I doubt whether Mrs Drummond"—and I emphasized the 'Mrs'— "would really be interested in selling."

Bill stood up. I shook hands with Mr Cooper, and walked her firmly out into the sunshine. She kept a straight face until we were well clear of the store. Then she let out a rich chuckle.

"Nice going, Mark. Some act you put on back there. That old son of a Martian coot was all set to call the town marshall."

I glowered at her.

"That was no act," I snapped. "I ought to put you across my knee and whale into you."

If that was meant to intimidate her, it didn't succeed too well.

"Lovely," she sparkled. "But not here. Let's go to your place and do it."

"Just shut up and follow me."

There was a striped umbrella joint just around the corner, where people sit outside to drink and watch the world go by. They serve good California wines there. I plonked her down at a vacant table and signalled the waiter.

"Anybody else who wanted to unload a gun would go to a hockshop," I told her. "There must be fifty places around here where you could have walked in, and no questions asked. But not you. Not the daughter of one of the famous Towers girls. You have to march into the most respectable place on the entire coast. Do you realise how much trouble you could have been in? How much embarrassment you would have caused your mother?"

She shrugged, unrepentant. From her viewpoint, she probably thought I was over-playing the heavy. I had to remind myself that she could not be aware of all the implications. Of the disaster that might follow if the police were to start asking questions at this particular time. But there were still some answers I wanted. Answers about the gun that was pressing uncomfortably against my side.

"You'd better tell me why you did this."

She looked surprised.

"That's fairly obvious, isn't it? For the money, naturally."

"Do they really keep you that short of money?"

"By Zeus they do," she assured me. "Shorter."

I was on the point of asking why she didn't get a job like everybody else, but I knew there were more important questions first.

"But why today?"

"I don't know. It could have been yesterday, or tomorrow for that matter."

"But it wasn't," I insisted. "It was today. The very day everyone is so upset on account of Uncle Tommy."

I was watching her very closely as I said it. The look of sudden astonishment appeared genuine enough.

"You know about Uncle Tommy? But we were supposed—"

Her words trailed away, and there was

worry on her face.

"What were you supposed to do?" I asked. "Keep it quiet?"

She waved an arm and sighed.

"Hell, this is difficult. Here's me supposed to be keeping a big dark secret, and there's you, shouting about it on the public streets."

"Don't exaggerate. Nobody's shouting. I'm talking to you privately. And you haven't told me why today. I'll tell you what I think. It seemed a good opportunity because of all the confusion caused when Uncle Tommy decided to disappear. Nobody was going to bother with an inventory of the local arsenal when they had so much on their minds. Would that be about right?"

Her look was unfriendly.

"You seemed to know so much. You figure it out."

"I'm trying. I'm also trying to keep my patience with you. Let me tell you something you don't know. Or don't seem to. Your mother brought me in on this Uncle Tommy disappearance. She looked for guns the minute he was missing. And she told me this gun had been stolen. Well, I say stolen. Taken away might be better. Only she thought her uncle had it. She didn't even think about you."

That seemed to have a little more effect on the girl.

"Oh. I—I didn't know that."

"So you tell me," I said nastily. "For all I know, it might have suited you very well. To have everyone thinking the old boy had stolen the gun."

"No, no, it wasn't that at all. Really it wasn't. It was simply that I needed some cash, and the whole place was in turmoil. It seemed an ideal opportunity. I never for a moment thought that mother would check, or that she'd blame Uncle Tommy."

She sounded sincere enough, but I still wasn't altogether satisfied.

"Then tell me one more thing. How does it come about that you managed to keep so cool during this family crisis? Or don't you care what happens to your uncle?"

That brought a flush to her cheeks, but not the kind I'd expected. This was caused by anger.

"How dare you?" she stormed. "I think the world of that old man. A damned sight more than anyone else in my precious family."

"Just the same," I insisted. "You managed to keep your head."

"Well, of course I did, after the initial

shock. There's nothing very new about all this. He's done it before."

That was something I hadn't known.

"Tell me about the other times. Please."

She sipped at the sparkling wine the waiter had placed in front of her.

"Not much to tell. He gets these fits, no I shouldn't says fits in case you misunderstand. Impulses would be better. He decides to take a break, and off he goes. Usually, he comes back inside a couple of days. It's no big deal."

"Where does he go?"

"I don't think I'm going to tell you that. He never explains to the others. I'm the only one he confides in."

I stared at her grimly.

"Then you'd better confide in me."

"I don't see that I have to."

I patted at my pocket.

"You're forgetting this. I may still tell your mother what you did."

Bill looked affronted.

"But that's blackmail."

I nodded.

"So it is. Well?"

She hesitated.

"Will you repeat it?"

"That depends. Not if I think it's

irrelevant to the present circumstances."

"All right. He goes to the races."

"Palmtrees Track?"

"Yes. He used to be a great gambler, or so he says. To listen to Uncle Tommy you'd think he'd been practically everything at one time or another. So every now and then, he nips off, and that's where he goes."

"And he never explains, when he comes back?"

"No. He can be very cussed, when he chooses. But he always tells me."

I wondered if Bill Drummond would be acting quite so calmly if I told her there was no racing at Palmtrees that week. Then I remembered that there was the second gun to account for.

"One more thing, and then you'd better get off home. Is this gun the only item you wanted to sell today?"

She looked puzzled.

"Why yes, certainly. What makes you ask?"

"Oh nothing. Just wanted to be sure I had the whole story."

"Well, you have. Will you tell mother?"

"Probably not. But I can't guarantee it. You'd better get back now. And no more crazy stunts like this."

"O.K."

We stood up.

"Er, I don't really have much to do. Couldn't I come with you? We could find some way of passing the time."

I grinned down at her.

"I have to get back to the office."

"I could come and wait for you. Make some coffee or something."

The deep eyes danced at me.

"Come if you want. I have an appointment with your mother at three o'clock."

That wiped the smile off.

"You're putting me on."

"Not this trip."

"I suddenly remembered an urgent appointment."

"What a pity."

As I paid the bill, she disappeared down the street. Damn.

I was stuck with the gun.

CHAPTER 7

I made it back to the office with four minutes in hand. Florence was missing from her desk again, but there were voices coming from my own room. Opening the door, I saw Angela Drummond enthroned in my best visitor's chair, while the Digby sat back against the top of my desk, leaning towards the client. They were jabbering away like two pillars of the community at a sale of work, and both looked at the intruder without visible pleasure.

"Ah, Mr Preston," greeted Angie. "I trust you have not shortened your luncheon break too severely on my account?"

Florence's face was impassive, but I knew whose side she'd be rooting for. I could have said I'd been too busy keeping somebody's daughter out of jail to find time for lunch. What I did say was,

"Oh no. I seldom exceed two hours. I see Miss Digby has been taking care of you."

"Most capably, thank you."

The Digby walked past me to the door.

99

"I'd better get back now," she said.

I took my time about settling behind the desk. It gave me an opportunity to gather my thoughts. It also allowed a few moments for an inspection of Angela Drummond, who was well worthy of the time spent.

She wore a rainbow splashed blouse in Japanese silk with full-length sleeves and high collar, along with immaculate white slacks in the same material. The hair was piled up today, in a way oddly reminiscent of her daughter's, but without the meat skewer. The more I saw of this woman, the more I understood what Society Charles Churchman meant about the Towers girls. Or at least, one of them.

Well aware of my scrutiny, she sat upright in her chair, and returned the favour. She was getting the worst of the deal.

"Your secretary, Miss Digby," she opened, "appears to me a most excellent person. Quite different from what one would have imagined."

What she meant was that a gum-chewing blonde, with a low neckline and an I.Q. to match, would have been more appropriate for somebody in my line of work. Particularly if the somebody was me. I resisted the impulse to bite back. My client was going to need her mental reserves for the interview that was about to take place.

"I'm very lucky to have her," I conceded. "Did she offer you some coffee, or a cool drink?"

"She did, thank you, and I declined."

In other words, let's get on with it.

"First of all, Mrs Drummond, were you able to make an appointment with your accountant, Mr Hawke?"

"Four o'clock," she confirmed. "He is a very busy man, and I'm afraid the time was not particularly convenient. However, I have been a client for many years. And, of course, he looked after my mother's affairs before that."

Great. He'd have to be a hundred and two years old.

"Good. Then we had better not waste the time we have. I have news of your uncle, and I'm afraid you must be prepared for something of a shock."

The violet eyes widened almost imperceptibly.

"Has something—bad—happened to him?"

"He is perfectly well, so far as I know," I assured her. "But let me tell you about my visitor."

I described what had happened when the large Mr Small had come to see me. She listened with a straight face, and didn't interrupt me once. When I was finished she clasped her hands together and inspected them for long seconds. Her voice, when she finally spoke, was quite controlled.

"An appalling story. Do you think it's true?"

Of the many questions I'd been expecting, that one was not on the list.

"That's an odd reaction, Mrs Drummond. What makes you think it may not be true?"

She pursed her lips and I realised she was having more trouble in controlling herself than had seemed at first.

"Because it's so far-fetched," she replied. "Kidnapping, threats of murder. Not to mention this so-called jewellery. A harmless old man wanders off, and the next thing that happens is this—this B picture plot. You must admit it doesn't ring very true."

If she was hoping I was going to agree with her, she was out of luck.

"I'm sorry, Mrs Drummond, but I don't admit to anything of the kind. It all sounds authentic to me. I think we're going to have to proceed on that assumption. Besides—"

"And the two guns?" She pointed a

triumphant finger. "What about them? Uncle Tommy may be a trifle foolish at times, but he isn't senile. If these so-called kidnappers had threatened him, he's not the man to crumple up and give in. Not with weapons in his pockets."

That was a valid objection from where she sat. My only real counter to it would have been to tell her that her own daughter had stolen one of the guns to my certain knowledge. An argument I couldn't use.

"I'm sure he's not," I said placatingly, "but we are dealing with determined people here. Your uncle probably even didn't realise there was any hint of danger until it was too late. And Mrs Drummond, there's one thing we have to remember. This story has to be true, because there is no alternative."

I paused, to be certain she was listening to me, and not off chasing her private thoughts. I needn't have worried.

"What do you mean, by saying there is no alternative?"

"I mean, because of who your uncle is," I explained. "He lives out there with just the family. He has no social life outside the house. You found he was missing, only this morning. Outside of myself, who did you tell about that?"

She looked mystified.

"Tell? Why, no one. There isn't anyone to tell."

Good.

"Exactly. That's my whole point. Nobody knows he's missing, therefore nobody can invent a story about his being kidnapped. That's one point. The other point is, the jewellery. That is not part of any story. That is a fact."

I reached inside my pocket. Angela Drummond watched as I shook out the small stone my recent visitor had deposited with me.

"This is the diamond the kidnappers prised from his watch."

She didn't bother to look very closely.

"Glass. I know the watch they're talking about,"—the reference to 'they' showed she was beginning to accept the idea—"it has about ten or possibly twelve of those glass fragments inserted round the casing."

Picking up the glittering 'glass', I held it out to her.

"Mrs Drummond, please. Won't you at least look at it?"

While she didn't exactly toss her head, she managed to convey the same impression.

"Oh very well."

Placing it in her palm, she gave it a cursory

glance. Then her expression altered slightly. She began to move her hand around in the sunlight. Orange, violet, yellow and red lights flashed from the stone.

"My God. Can it be possible?"

"I think it can," I replied. "We'll need a professional opinion, of course, unless you're satisfied without one?"

"No."

The reaction was emphatic, as she replaced the gem in front of me.

"They can do wonderful things these days. I like to think I can tell the quality of precious stones, but in a matter so important as this, I have no intention of standing on my vanity. We need a professional, as you say."

We were beginning to make some progress. Angela had moved quite a long way from her original flat rebuttal of the whole story.

"Now that you've seen this, how do you feel about the situation?"

"I don't know," she confessed. "It's all too preposterous. If that thing is real, and having seen it, I admit the possibility, then I suppose we would have to accept that the rest of his jewellery is also real. And that is not easy for me to do. Uncle Tommy had to part with all his pieces, one at a time, to pay for his many excesses. Gambling debts, mainly. I just don't see how he could ever have replaced them, especially without my knowledge."

"Gambling is an up-and-down affair," I reminded her. "His luck may have improved over the years."

She was staring at the floor, as though battling with unwelcome thoughts. When she spoke again, her voice was lower.

"Yes, but it goes beyond that, Mr Preston. During these same years, things have not gone well for the family. There have had to be many sacrifices. My uncle was well aware of what was happening. When he's lucid, he's nobody's fool. It is very difficult for me to accept that despite that, despite what he could see all around him, he could deliberately set about replacing his baubles, knowing full well how things were. I can't believe that of him. He should have shared with us, the way we've always shared with him."

It's seldom easy for people to accept cold-blooded selfishness from a close relative. For somebody in the people business, like me, it was all too familiar a story. My opinion of Uncle Tommy dived a couple of points.

"I think we are going to have to take it as a fact," I said, keeping my voice free of inflexion. "The insurance question is of paramount importance, but we'll have to leave that until we see Mr Hawke. That leaves the question of the money."

She brought her mind back to the subject in hand.

"Money? You mean the extra fifty thousand dollars these people are asking?"

"Yes. Can you raise it?"

Her shoulders had been slumped, almost in defeat. Now, she seemed to make a conscious effort to return to her normal pose of command. Sitting bolt upright in the chair, she said coldly,

"Fifty thousand dollars? I should have the greatest difficulty in raising fifty thousand cents. The answer is no. There is no possibility.

I could tell from the set of her face, and her posture, that there would be no point in probing, at that moment. We should have to go through the whole thing again, in any case, when we saw Mr Hawke. For the present, we had a stalemate.

"Well, I don't see that we can progress this any further for the moment. We'd better think about getting over to Mr Hawke's office."

Angela made no attempt to move.

"Will you tell me something honestly?"

"Of course."

With the usual mental reservations I always make, when people ask me that.

"These men. The ones who are detaining my uncle. Do you think there's a chance they will kill him?

That was the question I'd been expecting. I knew there would be little point in making a lot of reassuring noises. Angela Drummond was too perceptive a lady to be fooled. In any case, I wouldn't really be doing her a favour.

"It would depend," I hedged. "As a rule, with people like this, you can't trust them an inch. Once they get their hands on the money, the victim's chances of a safe return are not high. Kidnapping is a federal offence, Mrs Drummond. That means the people responsible are not safe in any state in the Union. The risk of identification is a real one, and a chance they won't normally take."

"But you told me they said—"

"Yes I did. And with your uncle, there's just an outside chance of its being true. He would be a very undependable witness, wouldn't you agree?"

She nodded.

"I'm afraid he would. Particularly on one of his bad days. But an outside chance is better than none, isn't it?"

I didn't want her building her hopes too high.

"Better, yes. But still not good."

"And even then—"

She shook her head angrily, and stopped in mid-sentence.

"Even then?" I prompted.

Her short laugh rang hollow in the room.

"I was going to say, it's all idle speculation. Sitting here trying to forecast what might happen in a situation which can't arise anyway. There is no possibility of my being able to raise the money."

Which brought us back to where we were.

"Before we go, Mrs Drummond, you'd better tell me how much you want the accountant, Mr Hawke, to know. Your business with me is confidential, and it remains that way. But you must be aware that I'm now withholding knowledge of a crime from the police. That's an offence, and a serious one. Oh, you needn't look concerned. It goes with the job, and I'm quite used to it, up to a point. Your friend Mr Hawke may take a different line. If he does, I could be in a lot of trouble."

I was beginning to learn how to tell when she was really paying attention. This was one of the times.

"As to that, I really couldn't say. Not with complete certainty. Josiah has been a good friend for a long time. A confidant. But I must admit, there has never been a situation quite like this before. One thing you can rely on absolutely. Whatever he does, he'll do his utmost to protect my interests. We shall just have to trust him."

"With all of it?"

"All of it."

"Including the shooting of Napoleon?"

Angela drew a deep breath.

"Yes. It all seems to be part of the same thing, doesn't it? Indeed, it has to be. There's no other explanation."

It was no time for us to be arguing about that.

"Shall we go then?"

In my town there are two different set-ups for impressing the customers. One is the razzmatazz approach. This is where you rent a flock of rooms in the newest skydenter, carpet the place wall to wall and fill it with furniture that escaped from Apollo IV. Around this you drape some spaceage fauna, in the shape of a few nubile dames who may or may not have brains, plus a few deadpan young men with severe cuts, and a running monologue spattered with phrases like 'market-wise', 'situation-shaping' and so forth. This means you are practically into the twenty first century, and a customer would be out of his mind not to leave his business in your hands. Investment-wise.

The other approach is the covered waggon set-up. A few rooms in older buildings filled with dark, heavy furniture, and a general air of timelessness. In front of the thick flocked wallpaper you seat one or two ladies of uncertain years, with an aura of plain cooking and the spirit of '49. The visitor knows you are in the Heart of America. These people have always been right where they are. They always will be. Solid, dependable.

The firm of Hawke and Jepstow was square in the middle of category two. If a man was to believe the brass plate outside, they had been in the solid dependability business since the turn of the century. A rapid calculation told me that the woman who looked up from the desk as we entered would have been no more than a slip of a girl when the firm opened.

"Why, Mrs Drummond. What a nice surprise. We don't often see you down here these days. And how are all the family?"

That's what I meant. It was one of those

'how are all the family' set-ups. None of your hustle here. No space hardware. You knew your money would be safe, because the senior partner kept it in a locked tin box under his bed. Angela and Miss Stoutheart talked about relatives and remedies and recipes for a while. I stood around, holding the parcels, or so it felt.

"You're to go right in. Mr Hawke is expecting you."

Mr Hawke was something of a surprise. He was tall and lean, with a bronzed outdoor look. As he rose from his chair his immaculate powder-blue suit fell into creaseless perfection. There was fluffy white hair each side of his head, and the top was the same colour skin as his face.

"Angela, my dear."

He held out both his hands in affection, and she took them warmly. Then she surprised me by leaning across the desk and kissing him on the cheek.

"It was good of you to make time for us, Josiah."

"My dear girl, you know I will always do that. You must be Mr Preston, sir. How do you do."

We shook hands, and I let him take a good look at me.

"Mr Hawke."

He waved us into ready-placed chairs.

"I gather from what you said on the telephone that you're here on rather serious business," he opened.

"About as bad as it can be," confirmed Angela. "I think it might be best if Mr Preston explains it all."

"Ah yes."

He had another look at me, as he leaned back twiddling with a silver pencil. I waited for the green light.

"You seem to have the floor, Mr Preston."

I told the story, sticking strictly to facts, and keeping any thoughts and speculations of my own out of it. There was also no reference to Bill Drummond's little gun-pawning expedition. Josiah Hawke's face remained impassive throughout the entire recital, but he glanced occasionally at Angela, to see how she was taking it.

"That brings you up to date, Mr Hawke."

"I see."

He laid the pencil down, and pursed his lips.

"Have you tried to persuade Mrs Drummond to place this entire business in the hands of the proper authorities?"

"Not very hard," I admitted.

"Why not?"

"Because, for one thing, Mrs Drummond doesn't persuade too easily. And, for another, I'm not sure it's the wisest thing to do. Not at this point, anyway. After we've talked with you, we may have a different slant on the situation."

Angela butted in.

"We don't want the police, Josiah. All other considerations to one side, there isn't time for them to do anything useful. This is very much a family matter, and very urgent. In any case, it's all so hopeless."

"H'm."

Josiah Hawke may be playing to the gallery, and he may not. I couldn't make up my mind. But he certainly had all my attention. If he decided to pick up that ivory-mounted telephone in the next few minutes, I could be saying goodbye to my license.

"You realise Angie—" I noted the 'Angie'—"That you are asking me to compound a felony?"

She looked at him imploringly.

"Josiah, I had to come to you. There's nowhere else I could turn."

The wise face softened as he looked at her.

"It is no more than my plain duty to call

the police," he told her, "but let us put that to one side for the moment. You, Mr Preston, must be wondering why I even hesitate. Old established practice, pillar of the community, and so forth. It would appear to be the automatic action of someone like myself to send for the police."

The way he spoke gave me some hope that he might not be intending to do it.

"That would be what I would expect, in the ordinary way," I admitted.

"Exactly so. Then I must explain myself, if you are to feel able to trust me. You don't mind, Angela?"

She smiled, shaking her head.

"I know whatever you do will be for the best."

"I hope so." He turned back to me. "You see, my interest here goes beyond the professional. All the way back to my youth, in fact. I was deeply in love with Mrs Drummond's mother, always was. I do not propose to expand on that, but as a result I have come to be regarded as an ex-officio member of the family. A kind of honorary uncle to Mrs Drummond and her sister."

I smiled gravely.

"Thank you for telling me, Mr Hawke. It certainly helps me to understand better."

"Good. I hope it will do more. I hope it will persuade you that any advice I may give here will not be that of an outsider, but of someone personally involved. However, first things first. Let us look at one or two facts. First of all, this question of the insurance. Tommy's jewellery was itemised on the same policy as your own and Joanna's, Angie."

My client made a sad face.

"Long gone," she muttered.

"Precisely. The jewellery itself has not been in your possession now for some time. But, so far as the insurance goes, I have been exercising an uncle's prerogative for some years past. The annual payments on that policy have always been made."

Angela looked as puzzled as I felt.

"I don't understand. Why would you bother to do that?"

The old man's look was kind.

"A protective instinct, let's call it. Someone, somewhere, would quickly have got wind of such a news item. The Towers girls were always news in those days, when the money problems began. It would have made a juicy item for the newspapers. There's nothing some people relish more than to hear about the misfortunes of people in higher places. I did not intend that to be the case

116

here, certainly not for the sake of a few dollars, once per year. So I kept up the payments. It's been no more than a harmless deception, until now. Indeed, if this story of the man Small's is to be believed, then there is no longer any deception, the policy is valid."

I digested this slowly. The opportunity was provided by Angela Drummond, who had buried her face in a large lace handkerchief, and was sobbing quietly. After a while, she raised her head, and her face was softer than I'd ever seen it.

"Josiah, I—I simply don't know what to say."

"Then say nothing, my dear. Far the best thing."

I would have to go along with that, but not for sentimental reasons. The fewer people who knew about it the better. My only regret was that I should be one of the few. Because Mr Josiah Hawke, with his protective device of carrying the Drummond insurance cover, was to my mind taking an awful chance. The ins and outs of insurance law is not an area of which I claim any knowledge, but it seemed all wrong to me to be kidding the company there's a half-million-dollars at risk, when all the family could ante up was a handful of glass.

It was time to call the meeting to order.

"Well Mr Hawke, now that you've cleared that angle, the point is, do you think the company will go for the arrangement?"

I think he welcomed the change of pace. His tone was more brisk.

"It would not be right for me to be too positive about that, but I think we may have a good chance. My firm has done a great deal of business with this particular company over the years. I flatter myself that a recommendation from me will go a long way."

Looking at him, it was easy to believe that it would.

"You'll need this."

Reaching over, I placed the diamond in front of him.

"Thank you. I must say, it certainly seems a very handsome stone."

"If the comany are prepared to pay," I continued, "that still leaves the question of the other fifty thousand. Mrs Drummond doesn't think it's at all possible."

He inclined his head, and looked thoughtful.

"In terms of cash availability, access to funds and so forth, such a sum is entirely out of the reckoning. I'm sure Mrs Drummond will have made that quite clear."

"Why, of course it is, Josiah," she cut in. "You knew perfectly well—"

He held up a hand, like a traffic cop, and the verbal traffic stopped. Still addressing me, he continued,

"Nonetheless, there is a financial area against which Mrs Drummond has turned her back for so many years now that she has almost forgotten its existence. I refer to the value of the property itself."

That started her motor again.

"The Towers? But that's out of the question. We have always agreed, that whatever else has to be sacrificed, we would never touch the Towers."

This was clearly a private fight, and a time for watching, not joining. I watched.

"Angie" he went on patiently, "no one understands your position better than I, and no one respects it more highly. You could have sold the house years ago, moved into a more modest accommodation, and lived the life of a wealthy woman. But the Towers has been a symbol to you, and I could not begin to list the sacrifices you have made to retain it. One by one, the valuables have been disposed of, paintings, silver, even furniture items. This is painful for you to recall, I know, but this is a time when you can no longer patch up a cash-flow emergency with such short-term measures. The Towers has stood for so many things in the past. Dignity, position, the maintenance of a status quo. All these things. I have often said to you, particularly of recent years, that you could not sustain a heavy financial blow. In saying that, I was speaking in more mundane terms, such as our new taxation measures. There was no way I could foresee anything of this kind happening. But it has, and it makes the position quite clear. Hitherto you have been prepared to forgo many standards of comfort for the sake of preserving the Towers, many reductions in the family's way of life. But now, we have a new situation entirely. We are now talking of life itself. And when you think of it like that, the Towers ceases to be a symbol. It becomes a parcel of real estate, of bricks and mortar, and land. You cannot for a moment weigh these things in any serious balance with Tommy's life."

Although his tone was kind, there was no mistaking the steel in the old man's voice. He was saying enough was enough, and there was going to be no nonsense so far as he was concerned, when it came to saving Uncle Tommy's skin.

Angela Drummond heard him out, her head bowed.

"You're absolutely right, Josiah. I suppose I knew from the moment Mr Preston explained what had happened that this would be the outcome. I was just hoping against hope that there would be something, that you could find some way—" Her voice faltered. "But no, I can see it was no more than wishful thinking. What do you wish me to do?"

Mr Hawke was too trained a negotiator to show relief, but I could detect a faint easing of tension. The old man had expected more of an emotional battle than he was getting.

"Let us then look at the details. We can only consider the site in terms of development. In this day and age, the prospect of finding a private buyer who would be interested in purchasing the house itself is remote. As to the land value, I assess it in present day terms at three million dollars."

He said it quietly, but I heard him loud. So did Angela.

"Three million?" she echoed. "As much as that?"

"That is a minimum figure," he assured her. "If we should have more than one interested party, an auction could develop.

The figure would certainly be exceeded."

With three million dollars in reserve, it seemed to me there was an awful fuss being made about fifty thousand.

"Then surely, there's no problem?" I queried.

Mr Hawke's face was pained.

"In terms of simple arithmetic, no. In practical terms, and those terms would include the repayment of the loan, yes. Yes, there is a problem there. With interest charges as high as they are, Mrs Drummond could not meet the annual repayments."

It seemed ridiculous, but he was the accountant. I shrugged.

"Then what happens?"

He ignored me, and turned back to Angela.

"You are going to have to let me help. Over the years, so many years, you have refused me, and I have respected your position. This terrible business of Tommy's kidnapping changes things now. You must let me loan you the money. And before you begin to protest, let me assure you it will be on a business-like basis. The money will be owing to me, or to my heirs, as and when the Towers is disposed of, finally."

She looked mystified.

"But that could be years from now."

He almost twinkled.

"Then I shall have to learn to be patient, shan't I?"

Angela's eyes brimmed, and she pulled anxiously at the corners of her handkerchief. I kept very quiet. It was very still for a moment in that old, cloistered room. It was Hawke himself who finally broke the silence.

"It is settled then. Mr Preston, I wonder if you would mind leaving us for a moment? I should like a few moments alone with Mrs Drummond."

"Of course."

I got up and made for the door. To my surprise, he followed me.

"I will show you out."

In the outer office, he dropped his voice to a whisper.

"Forgive the little deception, Preston. It is you I wish to speak with privately. When these people contact you, make whatever arrangements are necessary. The money will be forthcoming."

I thought he was overlooking an important point.

"Suppose the insurance company won't play?"

"Whether they do or not," he said slowly,

"the money will be available. You may accept my word for that."

He was going to stand for the whole hundred thousand himself. Isobel Towers must have been quite a woman.

"Mrs Drummond won't like it," I protested, but not very strongly.

"She will never know. Not from me."

His eyebrows raised in enquiry. It was a question.

"Nor from me, Mr Hawke. My word on that."

He went back inside, and I waited to take my client back to her car.

CHAPTER 8

That evening, I took a few hours off. There was nothing useful I could be doing in the Drummond case, and the next move had to come from the opposition. I went to Lee Moon's joint, and took aboard a helping of the Peking Special, along with a glass or two of that smokey-flavoured Chinese wine. I never can pronounce the name on the label, but the very small print at the bottom says it's bottled in San Francisco, and you can't get more authentic Chinese than that.

After that, I took in the new Woody Allen picture, and was back at Parkside by ten o'clock. An early night seemed a good idea, because the next day was going to be busy, and could involve working till the small hours for all I knew.

When I let myself into the apartment, the phone was clattering.

"Preston?"

A man's voice somehow familiar.

"Yes. Who is this?"

"Name of Small. You probably remember."

I became more alert.

"What can I do for you?"

He chuckled.

"Nothing yet. Don't get so impatient. We'll talk again tomorrow."

Then why the call, I wondered?

"You didn't phone to tell me that."

"No. Just a friendly chat. We like the way you're handling yourself. Been keeping kind of an eye on you. Just checking, you know."

They must be good. I hadn't spotted anybody. But then, they would need to be good, I reminded myself. This was no nickel and dime operation.

"Nice to know you care," I said sourly.

"You know how it is," he replied cheerfully. "Like to keep in touch. No cops, for one thing. We like that."

"I'll keep my end," I assured him. "Just stick to yours."

"Don't worry about a thing. Did you have a good chat with Mr Hawke? He looks like a nice old guy."

It's not an enjoyable feeling, to know you're being watched.

"Don't you know?" I queried. "I would have thought your man was hiding in my pants pocket."

"More or less," he agreed. "Anyway, you seem to be doing O.K, I'll call you tomorrow."

"Why not tell me now?" I pressed. "We could get this thing cleaned up."

"How? Do you have the dough?"

"Not yet," I admitted.

"Then we don't have a thing to talk about."

Sensing that he was about to hang up, I said,

"Hold it. How's my Uncle Tommy?"

"The old goat is fine. Don't worry about him. But you'd better help us tomorrow, before he drinks all the profits. Never seen such a thirst."

At least it sounded as if there was no need to worry. For the moment.

"If anything happens to that old man—" I threatened.

"Stop making noises. Nothing's going to happen to him. Just keep your end. Everything will work out fine."

"Then I—" I began.

There was a click, and a familiar whining noise. I replaced the receiver and sat down thoughtfully, unstringing my tie. If the point of the call had been to give me something to think about, it had been successful. While my mind was darting this way and that, the phone blatted again. Maybe he'd forgotten something.

"Preston."

"Mr Mark Preston?"

A different voice entirely. A man, dry, precise, unfamiliar.

"Yes."

"We haven't met, Mr Preston, but I hope you will not mind my calling. My name is Cilento. Alexander Cilento."

The only Cilento I knew was pulling two to five for assault with a deadly weapon. Somehow, I doubted whether there was any connection.

"What can I do for you, Mr Cilento?"

"I am calling you at the suggestion of Mr Churchman."

"Charlie, or rather Charles Churchman?"

"The same," he agreed. "Mr Churchman has told me of your great interest in Isobel Towers. As president of the Appreciation Society, I was naturally delighted to hear this end—"

"Hold on, Mr Cilento," I interrupted. "What Appreciation Society?"

He was too excited to be offended.

"Why, the Isobel Towers Society, naturally. We have a strong membership, you know."

No, I didn't know. It was typical of Charlie Churchman to stick this nut onto me.

"Really?" I tried not to sound too offhand. "Well, I didn't know that."

"Oh yes, really, very strong indeed. But always delighted to hear of a new enthusiast. Have you recently moved into the area?"

That was a terrible thing to say. It destroy's a man's confidence in his reputation. Mr Cilento evidently did not read the crime pages.

"No, I've been around for a long time, Mr Cilento. I think perhaps Mr Churchman may have exaggerated—"

But he wasn't really listening.

"We meet every month, on the first Thursday. That is to say, in two days' time, so you won't have to do a lot of waiting before you're able to come along and meet everyone."

This was going to get out of hand, if I didn't stamp on it.

"Thursday? Oh, well that's too bad. It just happens I have this important meeting on Thursday. Some other time, maybe."

He paused then.

"Oh dear, well never mind. Come along if you can. I'll give you the address, and we shall all be hoping you can make it. In any case, there's a meeting every month, so no real harm done. I'll read out the address now."

He gave me a Bay End listing, and I made a point of not writing it down.

"Well, thanks for calling, Mr Cilento. Maybe I'll be in touch at some future time."

"I certainly hope so. What we normally do, we have a little discussion group first, and sometimes we actually have a guest speaker, you know. Someone who actually worked with Isobel. A director, a cameraman, a writer. Someone with personal involvement of that kind. After that, we run one of her pictures, as a general rule."

"It sounds fascinating—"

"Yes, and this month we're showing one of her very best, Still Waters House. You've probably seen it already many times, but it's well worth another look. And we have an extremely good print, with the Brophy ending."

"The Brophy ending," I repeated helplessly.

"Oh, I know," he rejoined, "some people prefer the revised ending, the one Edward J. Milner substituted. That was entirely a box-office move, and certainly it was successful, by financial standards. But we in the society think the original Brophy had more artistic integrity. You sounded just now as though you might disagree with that?"

He sounded almost plaintive.

"Oh no," I assured him hastily. "For me, it's Brophy every time."

"Oh good. I am so relieved. Frankly, there was a little disagreement on the point, not so long ago. Two people resigned their membership."

"Well, some people let themselves get carried away. Anyway, thank you for calling, Mr—" I almost said 'Brophy'—"Mr Cilento. And good luck with your meeting on

Thursday."

He made a couple more attempts to restart the conversation, but I wasn't about to play. When I finally had the receiver back where it belonged, I said a few words about Society Charles Churchman, and went to bed. There were no more calls.

The first telephone call came a little after ten the following morning.

"Preston?"

"Speaking."

"Have you got the merchandise?"

It was my friend Small.

"It's waiting for me to collect it."

"How soon can you have it back in your office?"

I looked at my watch, and made a rapid calculation, allowing for the street traffic at that hour.

"I could be back here by eleven."

"Do that. Now, listen carefully. Be sure and have a pencil handy when I call again. Our delivery instructions are very complicated, and we won't make allowances for mistakes. You write down what we tell you. Got that?"

"Got it."

"The next call clinches it. Be ready."

I was holding a dead phone. I reached over and switched off the recording machine. Personally, I have a lot of reservations about some of the hardware people used these days in my kind of work. Voice-prints are a comparatively new development, and I doubted whether the few clipped phrases I'd had from Small would be of much help. There was probably no existing record of his voice for comparison anyway. Still, I couldn't afford to ignore any possibility.

When I got to Josiah Hawke's office, two hardfaced characters stared at me from opposite sides of the room.

"Good morning, Mr Preston," greeted the accountant. "These gentlemen are bank security officers. The banks seems to fear for my safety until I hand over the money."

"I'm glad to hear it," I told him. "I would have had a hell of a job explaining that the money wasn't ready because you'd been robbed."

The guards exchanged glances, but said nothing.

"I imagine there has been a—development?"

He was choosing his words with care.

"Yes, Mr Hawke. If we could be alone, I'd explain it to you."

"Of course. Gentlemen, thank you for your protection. Mr Preston will be taking the money when he leaves. I need not detain you any further."

They didn't like it. They didn't like me either. What they would have liked was an explanation as to just what the hell was going on. But they had their instructions, and Hawke's tone was quite firm. Treating themselves to one last hostile glance at me, they went out.

"Sorry about that," the old man said, "but the bank was most insistent. Well, what have you heard?"

I told him what Small had said.

"H'm. It sounds as though you'll have to go through some intricate manoeuvres to effect the handover."

"Yes," I agreed. "You have to look at it from their point of view. They can't afford to take any chances. I don't have to tell you Mr Hawke that kidnapping is a federal offence. The trickiest part of the whole deal is handing over the money. They've got to come up with something good if they're to avoid detection."

"H'm."

He pointed to a corner of the room, where a large brown suitcase rested.

"The money is in there. It's damnably heavy, by the way. You won't relish carrying it very far."

I nodded.

"They'll know that. I'll just have to hope they've allowed for it."

"You must realise, Mr Preston, how much all this goes against the grain," he said in a low voice. "Every instinct tells me to have you followed by half a dozen men."

"Certainly it does," I agreed. "I know the feeling. But it wouldn't do any good. Even the guy who collects the money will probably be no more than a courier. The important thing is to have Mr Towers freed, and that won't happen if there's any trouble."

"You really think they would kill him?"

"Yes I do."

"Very well. Then I must leave you to carry on."

He was right about the suitcase. It was heavy as hell. The two security men were loitering around outside. Although they didn't acknowledge me, they watched carefully as I heaved the bag into the car. So far as I could tell, I was not followed back to the office.

"My word, that looks heavy," greeted Florence Digby. "Tell me, are you going somewhere? Your other suitcase is in your office."

"What other suitcase?"

"Why, the one the delivery man brought. He said you'd be expecting it."

I went through to my own room. A large case stood in front of the desk, much the same size as the one I was carrying, but this was a heavier job, with steel corners. It was secured by a thick leather strap.

"Did you open it?" I queried.

"Certainly not. I think it's empty anyway."

I sprang the catches and looked inside. Nothing. No instructions, nothing. I didn't get it.

"When did this arrive?"

"Soon after you left. Why, is anything wrong?"

"Oh no, no. I'm expecting a telephone call, which will explain."

"Oh, I see."

Which meant she didn't see. I didn't see either. Not then. While I was waiting for my complicated instructions, I checked over the little electronic device for the hundredth time. This is a small circular piece of metal which gives off a signal at ten second intervals. The signal homes on to a control box up to a distance of one mile. The box was in my car. The idea was to plant the device with the money. That way, I could keep tabs on its movement, without being anywhere near the cash itself. The signal would exhaust itself within seventy two hours, but that should be time enough. Once the money changed hands, Uncle Tommy should be released. That was the deal. And once the old man was safe, I could see about getting back my employer's hundred thousand. I hadn't told anyone about the gadget, because in this kind of operation a committee of one is all that's needed.

Sharp at eleven, the phone buzzed. There were no preliminaries this time.

"Have you got it?"

"Yes."

"You should have a new suitcase in your office."

"It's here."

"Good. Now, did you get that pencil ready like I told you?"

"Waiting."

"First, you put the money in the new bag. Then open your office window, to show it's been done. I'll allow you ten minutes to finish the job."

I stared out into the street. It's always

comforting to know you're being watched. The phone went dead, and I got busy. A hundred thousand dollars in used notes is among the world's most beautiful sights. It is also a great deal of paper to shift. Kneeling on the floor, I began to transfer the wads of notes as fast as I could. I made it in eight minutes, and snapped the lid shut. Before buckling the big leather strap around it, I pressed my small metal circle inside it, at the base, where it wouldn't be found. Crossing to the window, I flung it open, for the benefit of my unseen observer. I even gave a little wave, to be certain I was noticed.

The telephone again.

"You seem to be co-operating well," said Small's voice. "Now, is that pencil ready?"

I had it in my hand.

"Ready," I confirmed.

"Pay careful attention. After I tell you what to do, I shall count five. Five, no more. No questions, no arguments. You do exactly what I tell you, or the deal's off. Kabish?"

"I'm listening," I confirmed. Listening, but puzzled.

"Lay down the pencil."

Thoroughly mystified now, I did as he said.

"Get up from the desk."

I stood, staring into the receiver as if hoping for clarification.

"Where's the suitcase?"

"Beside me, on the floor."

"Remember. A count of five. No leeway. Ready?"

"Ready."

"Pick up the bag, and drop it gently out the window. If you look out, you'll be shot. Do it now. One, Two."

Bending down, I scooped up the case, crossed quickly to the window and dropped it out. My office is two floors from the street level, and I could only pray the bag wouldn't drop on somebody's car. Worse still, somebody's head. But I wasn't going to risk getting shot to find out.

"I've done it," I reported.

But I was reporting to a whirring sound. Disgusted, I replaced the receiver. So much for the complicated directions. So much for the pencil. And so much for my homing signal. By the time I got down to the street and started my car moving, the money could be miles away.

There was no question about it.

I had been comprehensively had.

Reluctantly, I began to dial Josiah Hawke.

CHAPTER 9

Late that night, I sat in Sam's Bar, nursing my glass and brooding.

It had been an unsatisfactory case right along. I had done what was required of me, nobody got hurt, the client was satisfied. A more reasonable man would have deposited his face, and put the file away. But I don't like being made a fool of, and that was what friend Small and his buddies had done, so far as I was concerned. Well, I was out of it now, and there was no point in knocking my brains out. The thing to do was to forget it. I'd been on plenty of investigations where there were unexplained threads at the end, hadn't I? A person with my experience ought to know by now that these things happen. Life is not a neat parcel of simple explanations and obvious conclusions. It is a complex and baffling business, and a man ought to be grateful if he gets the final answer right, without expecting everything else to fall into obvious slots. The trouble with life is that it's complicated by the presence of people. If it wasn't for people, everything would be smooth. They are the cause of all unpredictables, the unexplained. But if a man is going to try straightening out people, then he'd better send for the guys in the white suits, because that's the way he's heading. The thing to do was to forget it, I reminded myself again. Close the file, take a few hours off, and wonder what the next case would bring.

Agreed?

O.K.

Fine.

That's settled then.

But dammit, I never even knew why Napoleon Scotsman the Fourth was shot. I'd been told who did it, but not why.

My mind ranged back again to that afternoon. The sunlight was picking up dust-motes in the peaceful room occupied by Josiah Hawke, accountant. It was four o'clock again, exactly twenty four hours since my first meeting with him. The case had just been warming up then. Now it was closed.

"It's good of you to be so prompt," he greeted.

I shrugged.

"I've had nothing else to do since I dumped the money. Except for one call from

Mrs Drummond, life hasn't exactly been busy."

He inspected me with wise eyes.

"Do I detect a note of disgruntlement?"

I must have sounded edgier than I'd intended.

"I don't know," I confessed. "I don't like this too well. I never like it when the bad guys win. That puts me with the losers, and it smarts."

"I detect a note of self-reproach. You have no cause for any such emotion. In my view, you have performed your part admirably. A view, I assure you, which is entirely shared by Mrs Drummond. Did she say anything on the telephone which made you think other-wise?"

"No," I admitted. "All she said was that Mr Towers was back, and then she thanked me, and asked if I would be in your office at four o'clock. I half-expected her to be here, by the way. Is she coming?"

He wagged his head sideways.

"No. She has left it with me to conclude matters with you."

Conclude matters? Did he mean I was being ditched?

"Could you explain that, Mr Hawke?"

"I intend to. Mrs Drummond has her

uncle safely back in the house. His jewellery was also returned, as per the bargain. She wishes to take no further action in the matter."

Just like that. I knew I'd have to keep a curb on my patience. If this was going to be my last involvement with the case, then at least I ought to find out as much as I could.

"Has the lady been able to learn anything from her uncle? Where they held him, and what they looked like, that kind of thing?"

Another shake of the head.

"I regret not. Tom was—not quite himself."

"You mean he was drunk."

The words came out before I could stop them. Hawke was not pleased.

"What makes you say that?"

"Because Small told me he was doing a lot of drinking."

The old man sighed, and spread his fingers.

"I see. Well, I'm sorry to say it is quite true. Indeed, and this is entirely for your ears, Tom Towers is not to be trusted, whenever there is alcohol available. It has been a family problem for years."

Great.

"So even when he comes to, he's not going

to be much help?" I pressed.

"Much help in doing what?"

I was surprised at the question.

"Why, in tracking these people down, naturally. I imagine you'll be bringing the police into this now?"

He pushed the heavy chair away from the desk, as if to increase his distance from me, and crossed one immaculate leg over the other.

"There will be no police," he informed me flatly.

Fine. And if I was also being eased out, that meant nothing whatever was going to be done.

"Mind if I ask why?"

"No. Indeed, I think you are entitled to an explanation. You have to try putting yourself in Mrs Drummond's shoes. She would dearly love to see these people brought to justice, as I would. But one has to consider the implications. You used an expression just now, the bad guys. Very well, let us use it by all means. You said the bad guys win, and therefore the good guys lose. In terms of an old morality play, that would be one way of looking at the situation. Unfortunately, life is not conducted in absolute terms. All black on one side, all white on the other, the forces of evil and good. If this matter was placed in the hands of the police, there is a possibility that they may trace those responsible. But at what cost? The innocent would be exposed, Mr Preston, had you thought of that?"

Since I had no idea what he was driving at, it wasn't hard to look puzzled.

"I don't follow that," I admitted.

"The family, man, the family," he said tetchily. "A household of women and one foolish old man, in a lonely spot. All publicised in the newspapers, with plenty of graphic detail. An open invitation to every burglar, even perhaps other kidnappers, or worse. You must be able to see that?"

Now that he spelled it out, it made sense.

"I see what you mean. Still, the police are very good at keeping things quiet, when they think it's necessary."

"Agreed, and I have every respect for them in that regard. But the newspapers are very good at finding out that something is being kept quiet. It makes them more inquisitive than ever. There is nothing more calculated to stir up a newspaperman than the feeling that something is being covered up."

That was true, and I couldn't deny it.

"So I'm being paid off."

It sounded ruder than I'd intended. I

waited to see whether he would take offense. To my surprise, his eyes twinkled.

"Mr Preston, let me tell you something. When Angela Drummond told me about you, I made a few enquiries. I won't bother you with names, nor with all the details of the reactions I had. Some of them, to be honest, were downright slanderous."

Slanderous, eh? I wished he wouldn't be so reticent with the names. But I said nothing.

"But, one or two things became clear. Everyone was agreed as to your honesty—" thank you kindly "—and also that you like to get results. The results often indicated some predilection for violence. Oh, you needn't look so offended. I'm sure it's sometimes necessary in your line of work. And I think it explains your present feelings."

"I'd like to know what you think those are, Mr Hawke."

"Certainly," he agreed, "and it brings us back to our morality play. I think you would like to go rampaging around the city, waving your gun, and beating information out of people, and daring the bad guys to meet you in Main Street at sundown."

I couldn't resist grinning at his image of Honest Sheriff Preston.

"You simplify things, Mr Hawke."

"A little," he conceded. "But not over-much, I fancy. You must not indulge yourself by becoming involved on a personal level." Here, his tone became very precise and professional. "Your position in this whole business is quite clear. You were employed by Mrs Drummond, for a specific purpose, which became overtaken by other events. You have played your role more than adequately, and now it is ended. The rights and wrongs of it are not your concern. You will oblige me by bearing that in mind."

So I was out of it. Indeed, if everybody else was going to drop the matter, there was no longer any 'it' to be involved in.

"Very well, Mr Hawke. I understand the position. It's all over."

"Good."

He thumbed back a folder on his desk, and lifted out a small piece of green paper.

"Here is a check for one thousand dollars. It is rather more than your minimum fee, but Mrs Drummond feels, and I agree, that you have more than earned it."

I took the check, and stood up.

"Well thank you Mr Hawke. I imagine I won't be seeing Mrs Drummond again?"

He rose from the chair.

"That won't be necessary. The lady wishes

to close this entire episode out of her mind. I'm sure you will understand.

I went to the door, then turned.

"I still feel bad about the dog," I said. "Is Mrs Drummond putting that out of her mind, as well?"

He shook his head sadly.

"I should have mentioned it. Poor Tom did that. He was probably drinking at the time, and it may have been the emotional reaction to what he'd done that made him run off in the first place."

"I see. Well, good day, Mr Hawke."

It was all very simple. Very straightforward. And, in those moments when I could think clearly, I had to admit the truth of everything the old man had said. None of it was really any of my put in. I'd done what was wanted, and I'd been paid.

It was over.

But here I was, hours later, sitting in a bar, and still chewing the whole thing through. The sensible thing to do was to forget it.

"How's that?"

A large beery man stuck his face close to mine.

"How's what?" I retorted.

"You said something about 'forget it'," he accused. "You're going off your chump,

147

pally?"

Talking to myself, I realised. This damned case had me talking to myself. The best place for me was home. I left some bills on the counter, and went home to bed.

I rolled in late the next day. There was nothing outstanding, and I'm no believer in sitting behind an empty desk for hours at a stretch.

"Morning, Florence."

The Digby treated me to one of her frosty inspections.

"Ah, there you are, Mr Preston. You will have been busy on the Drummond case, I imagine?"

Which was her way of asking why the hell I was so late.

"You imagine correctly. In fact, I have brought the case to the usual triumphant conclusion. Another victory for the well-known private investigator." I dived inside my wallet, and extracted the check. "There you are Florence. The reward of virtue."

She took it, shaking her head.

"I wish I'd been able to produce this at my session with the bank manager. Well, better late than never."

There's an old proverb that says an investigator is without honour in his own office.

"Any calls?"

"The railroad police have been on. A Sergeant Beecher. Do we know him?"

Beecher. Beecher. A bell rang very faintly.

"Sounds familiar. What does he want?"

Florence went very prim.

"Sam Thompson got himself into some kind of brawl down at the depot. They had to lock him up for the night. He's given your name as his employer."

"As his—? The nerve of that guy."

Thompson has done occasional work for me as a leg-man. If he could ever stick at it, he'd be one of the best in the business. Trouble is, he has this terrible thirst, and he hasn't time to spare for work, unless the bartenders are giving him those long-suffering looks about overdue bills. And now he expected me to get him out of hock.

Digby fixed me with a piercing glance.

"He's relying on you as a friend."

She made it sound like an accusation. As though it was my fault the jerk started throwing punches.

"Some kind of friend," I grumbled.

"If there's a fine, he could work it out, so many dollars to the hour. Shall I call Sergeant Beecher?"

I was being pushed around, and I knew why. If there is a crack in the Digby armour, it's something to do with Thompson. She's always a little too quick in his defence to suit me.

"Well, I suppose it'll do no harm to talk with him," I said, ungraciously.

The sergeant sounded a cheerful kind of man.

"You probably don't remember, but I met you one time at the ball-game. You were with John Rourke, of Homicide."

"Yes, sure," I lied. "How are you?"

"Just fine. We got a buddy of yours down here. He's a lot quieter today than he was last night."

"Is there a charge?"

"Naw. Let's call it one you owe the railroad."

At least I wouldn't have to pay anything.

"Thank you, sergeant I appreciate that. We must have a drink sometime."

"You bet."

I went back outside.

"They're releasing Thompson on the strength of my word," I told her. "Any more trouble and they'll throw the book at him. When he calls in, all full of gratitude, you can tell him I deserve every bit of it."

150

"Thank you, Mr Preston. I know how much trouble you went to. Exactly how much. You left your door open while you were talking."

Blast the woman. I grouched back to my own desk. Twenty minutes later, I was busy doing some highly technical research on the ponies lined up for Palmtrees at the weekend, when the phone rang.

"Is that you, Mark?"

Bill Drummond, and whispering. I groaned inwardly.

"Look Bill, I'm pretty tied up right now."

She ignored that entirely.

"Say, my respected mother tells me you buttoned up the whole deal, whatever it was. You move fast. Do you have any inter-galactic blood?"

"Just the red kind," I assured her. "Why are you whispering?"

"Because this house is crawling with the nosiest people," she breathed. "They even listen on extensions sometimes. Maybe now, for all I know."

"Then we'd better keep it short," I advised. "What can I do for you?"

"I'm not going to be too specific," she said guardedly, "but if you're not coming out to the house any more, there's a little item of mine you'll be wanting to return somehow."

Item? The gun, I'd forgotten about the gun. And she was right, I couldn't risk referring it on the phone.

"Oh yes, your—er—your lipstick. It's here in the office. Any time you're in town, just drop in. If I'm not here, my secretary will know where—"

'That won't do, I'm afraid. It's a special shade and I need it right away. Can you meet me?"

I didn't want to, on the one hand. But I did want to be rid of the Webley, on the other.

"I could make it some time this afternoon, I guess."

"Four o'clock."

"No." Four o'clock was not my favourite time for Drummonds. "Make it three."

"Where?"

"The reservoir on Canyon Drive. There are some rare water-birds out there at this time of year."

"Great. I'll wear my bird-watching suit."

I got there a few minutes early, and sat with the hood open, enjoying the sparkling water in the afternoon sun. A small green Toyota came into view, and was soon sliding into place beside me.

If that was Bill Drummond's bird-watching suit, they'd have to be very small birds. It consisted of one strip of material hitched over here and here, and a second strip stretched around down there. She sprang over the side of the car without opening the door, and poised to be admired.

"You like me, huh?"

"I don't know that liking would come into it," I replied.

She leaned on the door, staring down at me.

"You look as if you could eat me," she accused. "Wanta try?"

"Too soon after lunch," I demurred, though the idea was not without appeal.

"You have about as much sex drive as a Plutonian wimble-worm," she sneered.

"That's bad, huh?"

"The bottom line" she confirmed. "I can't imagine why Joanna thinks you're so special."

I found myself interested, without wanting to be.

"Why, what did she say?"

She tossed her head, the way a child would in a fit of pique.

"Maybe I won't tell you."

"So don't tell me. How's Uncle Tommy?"

"He's fine, I guess. Do you really want me

to tell you?"

"About Uncle Tommy?"

"No, dammit, about Joanna."

"Why not. Go ahead and tell me."

She looked all around, like a conspirator in an old-fashioned meller. There was no one else within miles.

"Joanna thinks you're on her side. That you'll help her in the big showdown with my ma."

Showdown?

"Oh. Is there going to be one?"

As I said, I was conscious of wanting to know. The girl grinned.

"Oh sure. One day. That's what Joanna always says, anyway. 'One day, Isabella, there will be a showdown. Then we'll see what's what and who's who around here'. She's been saying it since I was the size of an apple-pip."

It was an unfortunate comparison. Before I could stop myself, I said,

"That's a long time ago. You're a big apple now."

She pouted.

"I offered you a bit just now, and you turned me down."

I switched subjects, to restore the situation.

"So you're really Isabella. It's a nice name. Why doesn't anybody use it?"

"Oh, they do sometimes. When they're mad mostly. I mean mad-angry, not mad-crazy. They're mad-crazy most of the time."

I didn't want to hear any more. The whole family had a streak of the screwball so far as I could make out. They were nothing to do with me, and it would be best kept that way.

Opening the glove compartment, I took out the Webley.

"Will you be able to smuggle this back into the house?"

She took it and checked the chamber.

"You emptied it," she accused.

"I feel safer that way. And you didn't answer my question."

The handsome tanned shoulders shrugged.

"Oh sure. I guess. I got it out all right, didn't I?"

"Yes." Then I had another thought. "Your mother will know now that her uncle didn't have the gun. How will you account for it?"

"I won't try. I'll just stick it in some inaccessible place. Maybe it won't be found for years. Nobody will care by then."

"Uh huh." That sounded reasonable. "But the other gun that was missing. Still no sign of that?"

"Not so far as I know. It's probably mother's fault. She can be very careless about things that don't matter to her."

There was a wealth of bitterness behind her last words. I resisted the temptation to elaborate on the point.

"Well, I guess that's it, Isabella."

She started at the use of her full name.

"Don't look so surprised," I grinned. "It should make a pleasant change to have someone use your proper name when they're not mad."

I was dismayed to see the sudden tears in her eyes. She leaned quickly in, and kissed me. "You're nice, really nice. Take some advice from an old apple-pip. Stay away from us, Mark. We're bad news."

And she was gone. I watched the little green car disappear into the heat haze, then started the motor.

What had she meant by that?

Probably I'd never know.

CHAPTER 10

At seven that evening I walked into the welcome cool of the Trail's End. On my return from meeting Bill—now Isabella—Drummond, I'd found that Society Charles Churchman had left a message for me. It said that he hadn't seen me in an age, and that if I happened to be in the vicinity of his favourite spa that evening, he'd be glad to buy me a drink. I was intrigued on two counts. In the first place it had only been two or three days since we met, and that doesn't amount to an age. In the second place, Charlie Churchman had never bought anybody a drink within living memory, and it was not an occasion I would want to miss. You'd think at my age a man would learn.

He was parked on his usual stool, looking an advertisement for the world's best-dressed man. We were all in lavender today, even to the froth of silk which burst from the top pocket of his jacket with careful carelessness.

"Ah Preston, well met."

"Lo Charlie. You wanted to see me?"

I parked alongside him. The smell was lavender too.

"I simply thought it would make a welcome change for you to spend a little time in civilised company. You must get just the teeniest bit bored with all those gangsters and prize-fighters and the other riff-raff of your trade."

It's difficult to take offense with somebody so many light years away from reality.

"This is certainly different," I admitted. "Something was said about a drink?"

He ignored that entirely.

"Now then, do bring me up to date on the Towers girls," he begged.

"Nothing to tell. Anyway, I won't be seeing them any more. My little bit of business there—my very little bit of business there—is over and done."

He pouted.

"What do you think of them? Are they still as lovely?"

"Well," I hesitated, "a lot of years have gone by, Charlie. I would say Angela has weathered them better than Joanna."

"Fascinating. But you must be able to see what a splendid pair they made in the past?"

"Just the occasional glimpse, yes."

He glanced at his watch for the third time,

and looked at the doorway.

"Tell me, Preston, do you have an engagement this evening?"

"No. I thought I'd just roam around this great city and let it happen."

"Splendid, splendid. Ah."

His face registered relief. I turned my head, to see a dry-looking character approaching. He was about fifty years old, with wispy sand-coloured hair, and gold-rimmed spectacles that bobbed around as he walked.

"Good evening, Mr Churchman, I trust I'm not late?"

He spoke to Charlie, but it was me he was looking at.

"Not a jot, not a jot," chortled my betrayer. "You two have spoken on the telephone, I believe. Mark Preston, Alexander Cilento."

The man stuck out a bony hand, and I shook it. Cilento. This was the clown from the Isobel Towers Appreciation Society. I began to get a sinking feeling.

"The greatest possible piece of luck," enthused Charlie. "Mr Preston has just confirmed that his other arrangements for this evening have fallen through."

Cilento was all smiles.

"But this is good news. Then you'll be able to come along after all."

"Come along?" I repeated feebly.

"To the meeting," he explained. "This is Thursday. You remember we spoke about it?"

"Oh sure. I remember. Yes, of course I do. Charlie—" I turned a pleading face towards him, but I was going to get no help there.

"Well now, this is famous. And Mr Cilento has a little extra item for you, I believe?"

My new friend beamed.

"Yes, indeed. Mr Churchman mentioned your particular interest in Miss Towers' daughters. I've been able to locate an old newsreel which has a lot of footage about them."

I contrived a sickly kind of grin. There was no doubt Churchman had slammed the gate on me. Escape was not going to be possible. Still, I had to admit it would be interesting to see Angela and Joanna the way they once were.

"I should like to see that very much."

"Capital, capital. Of course, it will cut into our discussion time, I'm afraid. The meetings are never permitted to exceed two hours. A long-standing rule."

Some far-sighted committee member must

160

have known I was going to be press-ganged one day. I thanked him silently.

"My, my, look at the time. We shall have to be off."

I slid off the stool. Churchman stayed where he was.

"You heard the man," I said coldly.

"Yes indeed, most certainly," he replied in his blandest tone. "Sorry to lose you so quickly."

"You mean you're not coming?" I demanded incredulously.

A regretful gesture with his arm.

"Alas, I have a host of appointments this evening. I envy you, Preston, I really do."

And he still hadn't bought me that drink.

Alexander Cilento lived in style at Bay End. Not exactly millionaire country, but well up in the high-credit brackets. The meeting was to be held in the living room, a spacious comfortable area, where half a dozen people were already assembled when we arrived. I said hallo to Mr This and Mrs That, watching unmemorable faces swim in and out of view. Other people arrived, and there was more smiling and bobbing. Finally, there must have been about twenty people present, all anxious to get a look at the new recruit.

Out of the hubbub, a mellow voice whispered in my ear.

"You look like a man who needs a drink. I hope scotch is all right."

I turned gratefully to the newcomer, taking the extended glass. She was five seven, with the blackest black hair sweeping down either side of a long oval face. Bare arms were tanned the colour of honey, while the rest of her was covered from throat to toe-level in one of those silk gowns they wear in India. That's like in India, India, not India, Indiana.

"Scotch will be fine, and thank you. I don't think we've met. My name is Mark Preston."

"Yes, I know. My father told me about you."

"Your father?"

"The man who brought you. I'm Claire Cilento."

There was amusement in the dark blue eyes, and a hint of something else. Something I was afraid might be mockery. I sipped at the drink, searching for the right formula.

"This is good," I acknowledged. "Tell me, are you a member of the society, or are you just helping your father entertain people?"

"You didn't do that very well," she

162

accused. "You mean, am I here on sufferance, or am I one of these nuts?"

That was exactly what I'd meant, but I hadn't intended it to sound that way.

"Why not at all," I denied lamely. "What I meant was—"

"I know what you meant. Anyway, you first. How does it happen that our famous private eye develops a sudden passion for dear old Isobel?"

Her father and I hadn't discussed what I did to earn a crust.

"You know who I am, then?"

"I'm a crime buff," she confessed. "Are you trying to pin something on one of these people?"

I grinned.

"Hardly. I'm strictly a visitor. I happened to meet the daughters the other day, and it made me nosey. That's all there is to it."

Her teeth were very white against the brown-red lips.

"Then we're both phonies."

"Didn't I read somewhere that the phonies ought to stick together?" I suggested.

"We'll see. At this moment, I have to be about my duties."

She melted away, and I returned to the smiling and bobbing. Then her father came and took charge of me.

"We ought to be sitting down," he instructed. "If you would take that chair there, I'll just say a few words. Then I'll join you."

I took that chair there, and listened while he brought the crowd under control. Soon everyone was seated, and the lights were dimmed. Claire Cilento seemed to have vanished. A familiar beam twinkled from somewhere behind me, then the reassuring fanfare of Paramount newsreel crashed out, and there we were catching up on the latest in World War Two with the Nazis having things pretty much their own way in Europe. It was lucky I knew how things turned out, because I wouldn't have taken one to five on the chances of the French and British. Then there was some stuff about the new munitions plants which were springing to life on our section of the coastline. That really brought home the age of the picture, because half our lovely concrete was missing from the skyline. The last item brought the latest from Hollywood, and suddenly, there were the Towers girls. They were conducting an impromptu— ho hum—fashion show beside a marble swimming pool, and they were everything Charlie Churchman had claimed. I had to rely on the commentator to tell me which one was Angela, and which Joanna. Not that it mattered, each was a knockout in her own right, poising and smiling with practised ease. It was wierd, trying to connect these two with the people I'd been talking with only the day before. The soundtrack announced.

"And here's the son of a famous father, Napoleon Scotsman the Second."

A handsome Corgi dog appeared with the girls, who made a great fuss of him. I was sitting upright, because the dog was the image of his unlucky descendant, the one I'd seen dead in front of that fireplace. The newsreel came to an end, and Cilento turned to me.

"Well, how did you like it?"

"Fascinating" I admitted. "What did he mean, about the dog having a famous father?"

He looked surprised.

"Why, Napoleon Scotsman had a great vogue in Isobel's pictures. He was almost as famous as Rin Tin Tin, or Asta. People wrote him fan letters. Anyway, you'll be seeing him now. He appears a couple of times in 'Still Waters House'."

"Oh, That'll be interesting."

The main feature came on the screen.

Someone had added an orchestral soundtrack and a few sound effects, and so expert was the silent technique that I almost didn't notice the absence of dialogue.

Isobel Towers was a knockout. In the picture, she had returned from Europe to claim her inheritance, a gloomy old New England property, with the requisite banging shutters and lightning effects. Naturally, Bad Cousin Gus was trying to scare her away, but Handsome Harry was there to look out for her. So was his friend, a likeable bumbler who got bumped off in the second reel.

"That is Tom Towers, of course," whispered my host.

So I did get to see Uncle Tommy after all. A waft of perfume drifted over my shoulder. In the half-light, I could see Claire Cilento settling down beside me. Promising, but for now I wanted to see the picture. I knew there was something there, some extra fascination, and for a while it eluded me. Then I had it. It was the interior of the house. A lot of it was exactly the same as Isobel's Towers. At first I thought they must have shot the picture there, but there were differences. Finally, I decided that Isobel must have copied those features which appealed to her most, and had them incorporated when she built her own property. All the same, it was an eerie eighty minutes.

After the lights went up, I was still deep in thought. Then I realised Alex Cilento was speaking.

"You seem to have been quite absorbed."

"Eh? Oh, I'm sorry. It was the house," I explained. "It reminded me very much of her own house. Parts of it, anyway."

His face lit up.

"Ah yes. It would, naturally. You see, when she built the Towers, Isobel had them include the best features from several of the houses in her favourite pictures. You noticed no resemblance to the exterior, I imagine?"

Now that he came to mention it, no, I hadn't, and I said no.

"No, the outside appearance of Still Waters House did not appeal to her. For the outside, she used the house from her biggest success, The Millers of Mostyn Creek. I don't suppose you've seen that one?"

I walked into it.

"No, I haven't," I confessed.

He made a joyous little hand movement.

"Then I'll try to get it for next month."

I smiled weakly, and wondered whether the judge would be lenient when I assaulted Society Charles Churchman.

"Did you drive over, Mr Preston?"

Claire Cilento's voice pulled my thoughts away from red contemplation of the battered scribe.

"Yes, I did."

The silk thing they wear in India, India, rustled softly as she leaned across me.

"It's ten o'clock," she reminded her father, "and I have an early start tomorrow. Don't bother to leave your friends. I'll get Mr Preston to drop me off. If you don't mind, that is?"

Drop her off? Then she didn't live here. No, I didn't mind. It would have looked foolish for me to stand on my hands, so I contained the impulse.

"Not at all," I assured them both. "My pleasure."

We made our escape quickly, and soon we were heading back into town.

"Bet you have a gun in there."

She pointed to the glove compartment.

"You lose. It's under here."

I felt under the dash, where I keep a spare weapon taped in place in case of emergencies. She ran her own hand underneath.

"Lovely," she thrilled. "You're the first desperate character I've ever met in the flesh."

168

I grinned in the darkness.

"The only thing I'm ever desperate for is female companionship," I assured her.

"I'll bet," she retorted. "Anybody can tell you're the original sex-starved country boy."

"It's the straw. Gives me away every time. What's all the jargon about an early start tomorrow?"

She leaned her head back on the leather.

That's just to keep the aged parent quiet. He likes to have this image of me working myself to death. He still thinks I'm sixteen years old."

I took my eyes off the highway for an instant to look at her.

"I don't think you're sixteen."

Later that night, I mumbled in her ear, "This must have been what you meant, about meeting in the flesh."

She stirred lazily, running fingers down my spine.

"You're a phoney," she accused. "I still haven't found any straw."

"Keep checking around," I encouraged.

CHAPTER 11

When I let myself into the apartment it was almost three a.m. Although I was pleasantly tired, there was something nagging at the back of my mind, something to do with the picture show. For the past few hours, my thoughts had been elsewhere, but now they were beginning to straighten out again. I knew I wouldn't sleep properly with my head in a jumble, so I decided to take a nightcap, and spend a few quiet minutes before turning in.

I'd just located a clean glass when the door buzzer shrilled. A quick peek through the inspection hole, and I unfastened the locks.

Detective Second Grade Schultz of the Homicide Division stared at me in his blank-faced uncompromising way. I stared right back ditto.

"This had better be good, Schultzie. It's three o'clock in the morning."

"Why, so it is," he agreed. "I like your pyjamas, Preston. Neat."

Except that I'd slipped off my jacket, I was

170

still fully dressed.

"If you're selling tickets for the Policemans' Ball, you picked a helluva time," I grumbled.

"That was last month," he returned. "We missed you. Tell you what it is, we have a little identity parade going on, and the lieutenant thought maybe you could help us."

My astonishment was genuine.

"Identity parade? At this hour? Well now, you go and tell the lieutenant I'll be around in the morning. Ten o'clock sharp."

I made to close the door, but Schultz managed to get a large foot in the way.

"Don't give me a hard time," he begged. "Mr Rourke said to bring you. He said bring you nice, or bring you not nice, but bring you. Am I getting through?"

There was no mistaking the look on his face. Sometimes in life, a man stands up for his rights. Sometimes he puts on his jacket.

"I'll just get my jacket," I said sourly.

We took my car, and I made for police headquarters. My escort wouldn't tell me anything about the identity parade, and I gave up asking after the first few tries.

"Take a left here," he grunted suddenly.

"Left? Listen, I know the way—" I

argued.

"A left," he insisted. "We're not going to headquarters."

Mystified, I did as he asked. Twice more he gave me directions, then,

"This is it."

I pulled to a halt outside the city morgue.

"The morgue?" I protested. "One fine place for a show-up."

"Complain to the lieutenant," he suggested. "Let's go."

We went inside, to the bleak hygiene, and the over riding smell of chemicals. There was a group of men inside the attendant's office, most of whom I knew, at least by sight. There was one man I knew all too well.

Lieutenant John Rourke of Homicide glared at me from his battered Irish features, and looked enquiringly at Schultz.

"Did he give you an argument?" he demanded.

"Sweet like a bird," denied Schultz. "He was alredy dressed for the street. In fact I had to wait outside till he got home."

"Well, well." Rourke turned to me. "Out doing a little charity work, were we?"

It was no time of night for his heavy-handed humour.

"Spare me the gags, John," I begged.

172

"Let's take a look at these people."

"People?"

The fierce eyebrows shot up in enquiry at Schultz.

"I told him it's an identity parade."

"Ah." Rourke chuckled. Very briefly. "Well, that's right enough in a way. So it is. Come on, Preston. Let's get to it."

He led the way to one of my least favorite places. I'd guessed by now what was going on, and it didn't make me feel any better. The huge refrigerated file cabinets stared down at me from all sides.

"Number Seven," grunted Rourke.

The attendant grabbed at the handle, and the big drawer slid soundlessly outward. We all moved in, and I stared down at the still features of the late Mr Small.

"Mind telling us who he is?"

"I haven't the faintest idea," I shrugged.

It was true, too. All I knew was what he'd chosen to tell me, which may have been true, and then again it may not. And I was pretty certain of one thing. His name wasn't Small.

"Then how come he knew you?"

This wasn't the time for smart answers. It was a time for selecting words with care.

"Who says he knew me?"

"He does," Rourke assured me. "Take

173

another look, maybe it'll come back."

I leaned forward, not to take another look, but to give my mind a chance to assimilate this new information. What was there about this dead man which provided a link with me? Then I had it. His pockets, of course. There'd been a note, something written down. But what? And why was he dead, anyway? Although, with a hundred thousand dollars in the background, there could be plenty of answers to that.

Then I straightened again, shaking my head.

"No. I still don't know who he is. What happened to him?"

"Somebody shot him. Three times. Wasn't you, was it?"

It wasn't a serious question. If it had been, the asking would have taken place under very different circumstances.

"No, it wasn't me," I denied. "I never shoot strangers. Just the occasional friend or neighbour."

"What I figured," Rourke assented. "Take a look at his hand. This hand."

He pointed to Small's left.

I looked at the clean, well-tended fingers. Nothing. I shook my head.

"Try the palm."

Rourke nodded to the attendant, who grasped the dead man's arm, and turned the hand so that I could see the inside of his palm. There were faint blue remarks, such as a ball-point pen might make, but I couldn't make sense of them.

"What is it, a message?"

"Kind of. O.K., thanks. We've seen enough." He nodded to the attendant. "Let's go back in the office."

I think everyone was relieved to get back to more normal surroundings. By now, I'd decided it would look suspicious if I kept too quiet. After all, I had been dragged out of my home in the middle of the night.

"Look, John—" I began.

"Don't be so formal," he snapped. " 'Lieutenant' will do."

It wasn't a good sign.

"You know I always cooperate with the law—"

"—huh—"

"—but you'd better tell me where I'm supposed to fit in all this," I ploughed on. "Even a private badge has certain rights."

Rourke lit one of his foul little Spanish cigars, and blew yellow smoke at me.

"Oh sure, you have rights," he agreed. "You have a right to call a lawyer, if you want. You have a right to so many cubic feet of country earth, like your buddy in there. "

"He's not my buddy," I interjected.

"Maybe. Want to know where we found him?"

"If you want to tell me."

I tried not to sound too interested.

"Somebody dumped him in the old Fish Market. He could have been there for weeks. Nobody ever goes near the place, since it was shut down. As it happens, we got a break. There's a move afoot to redevelop that section. Some of our city planning people went down there, and found more than they bargained for."

I misunderstood him deliberately.

"You said he'd been there for weeks?"

Rourke made an impatient face.

"You don't listen very well, do you? I said he could have been. We got lucky, this time. He hadn't been dead much above twenty-four hours when they found him."

That would make it a matter of hours after the money was collected.

"And where do I come in?" I pressed.

"If I knew that," he said nastily, "I could lock you up, and we could all get some sleep. You saw his hand?"

"I saw those little marks. They meant

nothing to me."

Another cloud of stinging fumes drifted in my direction.

"John Doe was right-handed. Forensic noticed these ink marks on his left palm. They were faded, because the guy had washed his hands since he put them there, but a little work with the chemicals soon told them what the original had said. You know how it is with scraps of information. Some people scribble on cigarette packs, some on the back of an envelope. But if a man has no other surface to write on, sometimes he'll scribble inside his hand. That's what old John in there did."

The lieutenant paused, for effect. He needn't have bothered. I was hanging on to every word.

"So what did he write?" I asked, as casually as I could.

"He wrote down your telephone number, Preston. His pockets were empty. There was no wallet, no identification, nothing. Somebody went to a lot of trouble to prevent us from identifying this man. But they didn't think to look inside his palm. Who would? But there it was, plain to see. Your telephone number. Why would he make a note of that, do you suppose?"

But he'd talked too long, and I was getting more wide awake by the minute.

"Who says it's my number?" I demanded.

Rourke looked wide-eyed.

"Why, the City Directory seems to think it is. The Post Office seems to think it is. What are you claiming, a case of mistaken digitals?"

I shook my head.

"I'm not claiming anything. I'm saying you have nothing at all. A set of numbers. They happen to coincide with my telephone. In this town. With somebody else's phone in another town. Practically any town of any size. They could also be an army service number, a bank account number, a computer access number, I could go on all night. A lawyer could probably go on for a week." The longer I talked, the more confident I was getting. "All right, my telephone was one possiblility, out of hundreds. Like a good citizen, I cooperate to see if I can help you. Fine. But I can't. So you'd better move on to the next possibility on your very long list. Right now, I'm tired, and I'm going home. Are you going to try stopping me?"

He stared at me thoughtfully, and without rancor.

"That was interesting, that part about the

good citizen. You heard that, didn't you?"

He was talking to Schultz, who nodded.

"Got it, Lieutenant."

"And you heard this good citizen deny any knowledge of the dead man?"

"Right."

"You heard him talking about his rights, and lawyers, and all that stuff?"

"I did."

"And it'll all be in your report, won't it?"

Schultz wagged his head.

"You bet it will."

Rourke nodded, satisfied. "Yes. I'll just bet it will. Did you also hear me tell this good citizen that I'll bend a truncheon over his head if I find out he's lying to me?"

The detective shuffled his feet.

"No, I don't believe I caught that part, lieutenant."

"Ah. Or that I told him what he could do with his smart ass lawyers, if I so much as catch him with an overdue library book?"

"I couldn't have been listening when you said that," Schultzie grinned.

Rourke turned to me, glowing.

"You see, that's one of my problems. I get these incomplete reports from my own squad."

But it was over. The lieutenant was holding low cards.

"I'll be getting along. Tomorrow's going to be busy," I told him.

"Busy doing what?" he sniffed, suspiciously.

"I have to get all my books back to the library, before you put the dogs on me."

I went home to bed. This time there was no nightcap.

Next morning I called the office to say I'd be working from home for the rest of the day. Then I padded around, drinking endless cups of coffee, and pushing up the sales curve of the Old Favorites brand. Four times I went to the telephone, and four times I changed my mind. The murder of my acquaintance Mr Small had put me in a spot. He'd told me he was from out of town, and that was how he came to be elected as a contact man. That part of his story seemed to be borne out by the fact that the homicide people were having problems in identifying him. The most satisfactory reason for his death, from where I stood, was that he was eased out by his business partners. Edges get very blurred, and loyalties strained, when there's a great bag of untraceable cash at stake. It could have happened one of two ways. Either Mr Small got greedy, and wanted to take off for the hills with more than his share, or his buddies decided they didn't need him any more. If either of those possibilities was true, then I could close the file and forget it. The trouble was, I couldn't close my mind against other possibilities. That somehow, someone from Isobel's Towers had managed to trace the man, and took their own vengeance. There were guns enough to be had, as I well knew. Bill Drummond, for one, was always waving artillery and taking potshots. I didn't know whether she would have the stomach for an actual killing, but she was just kooky enough to make me wonder. And there was dear old Uncle Tommy. I'd never met the man, but I'd seen him the way he used to be, and he looked like a useful man in a brawl. Angela Drummond had volunteered that he wasn't the man to stand for being pushed around, old as he was. Supposing he'd suddenly sobered up, remembered where they'd been keeping him, and gone on the rampage? O.K. it wasn't very likely, and I was probably imagining the whole thing. About Bill, too. That was it. It had to be. Just my mind, rushing off in all directions, dreaming up fantasies. Best thing would be to forget it. That was the answer. It was good to have reached a positive decision.

Yes.

But I didn't dream up the image of Mr Small staring up at me from a slab in the morgue.

That was real. And those holes in him. Three, according to John Rourke. They were real. Somebody put them there. Maybe somebody I knew. Somebody I'd been talking to in the past few days. Or, in Uncle Tommy's case, talking about.

I could rationalise until I was black in the face, but my imagination refused to let it rest. If Mr Small had been murdered by someone from Isobel's Towers, I had to do something about it. There was no way I could live with myself, so long as I permitted the existence of that possibility.

It was none of my concern, anyway. I'd been hired to do a job, and I'd been paid off. What happened after that was nothing to do with me, was it? It was none of my business.

That's settled then.

Forget it.

Fine.

But murder is everybody's business. Nobody has the right to sit quietly by, letting other people roam around, snuffing out human life. What kind of a world would we have, if people let that sort of thing happen?

People like me.

It's all surmise. Conjecture. Guesswork, nothing more. There wasn't one positive lead I could point to. Not one tangible piece of evidence to which I could tie any of these outlandish theories.

Except Mr Small.

His tie-in with the Drummond household was positive and strong. And, in any case, there was no point in all this pussy-footing around. The only way to set the mind at rest was to go out there. To get out to the house, and talk to people. Ask questions, toss a little beef around, if necessary. Anything rather than this now-you-believe-it, now-you-don't, nonsense.

I didn't call from the apartment. It isn't that I necessarily believe all this stuff about wire-tapping, but there's no point in taking foolish chances. Instead I parked by the first pay-phone I reached, and dialled the house.

Angela Drummond answered quickly.

"This is Preston, Mrs Drummond, I have to see you right away."

She didn't welcome the idea with open arms.

"Oh? But I understood our—um—transaction was completed?"

"So did I," I assured her. "But something has come up. Something important."

Again she waited before replying.

"Obviously, you don't intend to discuss it on the telephone."

It was a statement, not a question.

"Can't be done," I confirmed.

"I will call Mr Hawke immediately," she decided, "He will—" "No," I bit rudely. "He's out, positively out. If what I'm afraid of is even halfway correct, then it's our job to protect Mr Hawke. Yours, more than mine."

"Protect—?" she began, then faltered away.

So far as I was concerned, old Josiah had done all he could to protect these people. I wasn't going to risk exposing him to an accessory-after-the-fact rap. And I was through arguing.

"I'll be out in thirty minutes," I told her, and replaced the receiver.

I was sick of the whole affair. Even now, I was taking a chance that nobody had any right to expect. My check had been deposited, none of this was any of my put-in.

The proper place for me and my half-baked notions was police headquarters. A few minutes later I passed beyond the city limits.

CHAPTER 12

It was about a mile away from Isobel's Towers that I first heard that noise. A high-pitched, insistent whining, repeated at short intervals. The obvious solution was some kind of signal being picked up by the radio, so I switched off the L.A. Jazz Festival with reluctance. That's the trouble with these outdoor live transmissions, there's so much competition for wave-space.

The noise was still there.

An electrical fault could be anywhere on that involved circuitry, I pushed buttons, and switched switches, and listened.

Beep—beep—beep.

Unclipping the hand extinguisher, I laid it beside me on the seat. Then I pulled gently into the side of the road and killed the motor.

The noise was coming from the rear seat. With comprehension came relief, as I reached back and pulled the picnic blanket clear.

I'd completely forgotten the little black box, but it hadn't forgotten its job. It was supposed to tell me when I was getting close to a certain suitcase. One with a hundred thousand dollars inside. And here I was, within one mile of Isobel's Towers. It could be coincidence, of course. The box operated to all points of the compass, within its given radius. Just the same, a man ought to look out for himself.

I drove to the next gas-station, and called Florence Digby. There was a job for Sam Thompson, and she would have to locate him urgently. Then I went to the lunch counter and ordered a cold beer, dawdling over it for the next twenty minutes. Thompson would have started by now. Time for me to finish my journey.

The iron gate was open this time, so I didn't have to stop. It could have only been my imagination, but the ragged trees seemed somehow sinister as I passed between them, and the house itself looked almost forbidding, despite the sunlight.

As I stepped from the car, I could sense I was being watched. Well, what about it? People often watch out for expected visitors. In the back of the car the little black box was going crazy. I switched it off and tucked it under my arm.

Joanna Towers opened the door at once. "Hallo," she said brightly. "Angie tried to tell me you wouldn't come to see us any more, but I knew you would."

Well, at least one person was glad of my visit.

"You're looking very well Miss Towers," I told her.

She simpered.

"Joanna please. You must call me Joanna. Everyone does, even Bill. That's my niece, you know."

"Yes, I've spoken with her. Is she here today?"

Hands fluttered out from her sides, and disappeared again.

"Oh, somewhere I guess. She'll be around the house," lowering her voice, she added, "you mustn't let her shoot you, you know. I think it's foolish, the way Angie lets her go around, waving those things."

"I'll be very careful," I promised, and I wasn't merely humouring her. "But I suppose I'd better get inside and talk to Mrs Drummond."

Her face dropped.

"Oh yes, I guess you had. Come in, come in. She's in the library."

Joanna bustled off as I made my way across the hall. I felt I was in familiar surroundings now. Not only had I been there before, but

I'd also watched Isobel Towers herself cavorting through the cardboard original.

Angela Drummond looked very severe, sitting in that tall chair, and fixing me with a glance that was far from friendly.

"I understood you to say thirty minutes, Mr Preston that was almost fifty minutes ago."

I looked apologetic.

"It was to do with the car," I explained.

At this stage in the conversation, I wasn't going to tell her exactly how the car came into it. And I noticed I wasn't invited to sit.

"You were very mysterious on the telephone. I must tell you that if it wasn't for what you said about the need to protect Mr Hawke, I should have refused to see you altogether. I regard the whole sordid business as a closed chapter."

"Well, since then, somebody got busy on chapter two," I snapped.

I wasn't going to stand around, like some wayward student being told off by the principal. Dragging a wooden chair behind me, I walked up close and parked myself.

"Go on, I gather there has been some development."

"You might call it that," I agreed. "The man who first came to see me was named

Small, you may remember."

"I do. What about him? Has he been in touch with you again?"

The smell of chemicals came back to me.

"In a way. I've just been down to the mortuary to identify him."

A hand flew up to her mouth.

"To id—are you saying the man is dead?"

"Very."

"But that is shocking," she said slowly, "I gathered from your description that he was quite a young man."

"Oh, he was. But even a young man is liable to get dead if somebody puts three bullet holes in him."

A gasp from behind the hand.

"You're telling me he was murdered, aren't you? That the other gangsters must have killed him for his share of the money?"

"It's a possibility," I agreed.

I left her to think about that, while I fished out an Old Favorite and set fire to it. Her glance was disapproving, but she didn't try to stop me.

"Mr Preston, I'm afraid you'll have to explain a little further," she informed me icily. "What other possibilities can there be?"

"We'll get back to that," I hedged. This conversation was going to be run my way, for a change. "Your first question should have been to ask how come I had to identify the body."

She agreed at once.

"But you are absolutely right. I hadn't thought of that. How on earth did the authorities manage to connect you with the man Small?"

"He was carrying my telephone numer," I explained.

I didn't explain where he carried it.

"Your telephone number?" she repeated. "Then, do the police think you had anything to do with his death?"

"Not really. They had to ask, but it was no more than routine."

I had the oddest feeling that Angela Drummond was merely going through the formality of conversation, because it was something people did. It was almost as if, had I decided to get up and walk out, she would have dismissed both me and Small from her mind. As though she was remote from the whole business, and didn't really want to be bothered with it.

"From the way you speak, I gather you managed to avoid involving the family?"

Even the question was dismissive.

"On the first trip, yes," I confirmed. "But

they'll be back. The police are going to have a lot of trouble identifying our Mr Small. I'm the only lead they have, so they'll come back again. Only harder, next time."

"Unless they catch the gangsters first," she reminded.

"If it was the gangsters."

She stopped her inspection of the far wall, and looked into my eyes.

"That's the second time you've said that. What does it mean?"

"It means this house is full of guns. It's also full of people who have no reason to love Mr Small. I want to know where everybody was yesterday, and the day before. You had better understand me, Mrs Drummond. You people have to satisfy me that this murder is nothing to do with the family, or I go to the police. I'll be in plenty of trouble as it is, but not nearly as much as if I try to hush up information on a murder."

That did it. She stood up, trembling, and pointing to the door.

"Get out of my house."

I sat still and smoked, looking at her. The pose would have looked good in one of her mother's old movies.

"I said, get out," she repeated, her voice rising.

"Sit down Mrs Drummond," I advised. "You haven't realised it yet, but I'm the nearest thing you have to a friend in this caper. I don't care too much about Small being dead. What I do care about is being satisfied he wasn't killed by someone here. All you have to do is satisfy me on that, and we can forget the whole thing."

The pointing arm faltered, then was lowered to her side. She stood there for a moment, irresolute, then crumpled gradually back into her seat.

"You don't, you can't possibly begin to understand," she said in a low voice. "It's the strain, the continual strain, day in and day out, of trying to care for all these people. The responsibility. Trying to keep them out of harm's way, wondering what they're up to every minute, afraid to let them out of my sight." She raised her head suddenly. "It must sound to you, a stranger, as though I'm whining. Well, I'm not. It's my job. There's no one else to do it, and therefore I must. But when you come in here with something like this, something unthinkable, it makes a mockery of all the years. I'm expressing myself badly, I'm sure."

There was no doubt she was suffering. I could see it must have been an awful strain looking after a houseful of kooks all those years.

"Mrs Drummond," I said, as gently as I could. "Try not to think of me as the man with the bad news. Quite the reverse. So long as you're dealing with me, you'll still have some measure of control. Once the police get here, that's out. Now, why don't we just get on with what we have to do?"

She took a deep breath while she regained control.

"Very well. It will be a waste of time, of course. Any such suggestion is utterly beyond the bounds of reason. Nevertheless," she ploughed on, seeing that I was about to interupt, "I can see your point of view. My choice seems to lie between setting your mind at rest, or dealing with the police. Given such a choice, there is no doubt as to which I prefer. How do you propose we proceed?"

I contrived to peek at my watch, without making it obvious. Sam Thompson couldn't arrive for another ten minutes, at best.

"Perhaps we could have a talk with your uncle?" I suggested.

Angela sighed.

"I don't know whether the poor man will be up to it. He's not been at all himself since he came back."

Stoned again, at a guess.

"I think we ought to try. Is he still wearing all that jewellery, by the way?"

She seemed surprised at the question.

"Jewellery?" Why, I hadn't thought about it. I mean, that is, he certainly was wearing it when he came home. He may have put it away since then, I really don't know."

I couldn't believe I was hearing it. A half million dollars worth, and she didn't know?

"I would have thought your first move would have been to get that stuff locked in a vault," I said. "Didn't Mr Hawke say anything about that?"

"Yes, yes he did. Naturally, he did. And I intend to do it. But the relief at seeing my uncle put everything else out of my head. I shall do it tomorrow, without fail. First thing tomorrow."

Ye gods.

"And what about the missing guns? Did he have those with him?"

I knew about the Webley, but I still didn't know the truth about the little purse-gun. Angela looked astonished.

"Do you know, I'd quite forgotten about those, with everything else that's been going on. I expect those men took them from him."

"Well we can ask him about that, too."

"I'll go and find him." She got up again, then looked at the box by my feet. "What is that, some kind of recording machine? I hope you're not recording all this?"

I made a gesture of denial.

"Oh no. Nothing like that."

"Then what is it? You haven't had it with you before."

She was standing four-square to me now, and wasn't going to leave until she had an answer. I checked my watch. Eight minutes.

"It's a little electronic machine," I hedged. "For tracing things."

It seemed to satisfy her.

"Ah. You mean the guns? It makes a clicking noise or something? I saw one on television once."

"That kind of thing," I mumbled.

"Fascinating. I'll go and look for Uncle Tommy. Would you mind pulling up a chair for him?"

"Not at all."

I still don't know how I could have been so clumsy.

Rising on the half-turn, my foot struck against the box, flipping it on its side.

Beep beep beep beep beep.

The signal was no longer merely insistent. It was practically frantic.

We both froze where we were.

The door to the inner room burst open. Bill Drummond came in fast, the Webley large in her hand.

I flinched against coming pain. She waved the gun at me.

"What the hell is that thing?" she demanded.

Angela ignored the question.

"For heaven's sake, will you put that thing down, girl? You know how nervous it makes me. How many times must I tell you?"

Bill winked at me and shrugged. I tried to wink back, but my face muscles were still frozen in fear. She put the gun down on the table. My sigh of relief was almost as loud as the noise from the box.

"Well?" she demanded. "Is someone going to answer me?"

Bending down, I flicked the switch over and the beeping stopped. Her mother said.

"What were you doing in there?"

"I was listening," replied Bill cheerfully. "Nobody will tell me what's going on around here. It was the only way I could find out. But I couldn't catch all of it. What about the box?"

Angela frowned her disapproval.

"If you must know it's a kind of tracing

machine. Mr Preston thought it might help him to locate the missing guns. And it certainly works, I must admit. That thing there must have set it off."

She pointed disdainfully at the desk.

Bill tossed her head.

"That's a load of Martian camel-waste," she scoffed.

"What does that mean?" demanded Angela.

"What I said." Bill looked at me searchingly. "I know about those metal detectors. They're not selective, they haven't any brains. Anything made of metal will set them off. Coins, nails, cutlery, anything. So you'll have to think up another one, Mark."

My employer came closer in.

"If that is true, Mr Preston, I think an explanation is called for. What exactly does that machine do?"

Six minutes to go.

I stared from one to the other.

"It's a homing device, like I said."

"But what does it home onto?" queried Bill.

Angela was beginning to show agitation.

"I don't think your mother will want me to discuss this in front of you."

We all took turns looking at each other.

Angela said,

"I think you'd better leave us, Bill."

More head-tossing.

"You and your big secrets. That's what they ought to call this joint. The House of Secrets."

"Will you go, please."

Bill heaved her shoulders, and made to pick up the Webley.

"And leave that thing where it is," commanded Angela.

A final sniff, and Bill stalked out through the hall door. When it was firmly closed, Angela looked at me.

"Well?"

"It was an idea I had, when we paid over the ransom money," I began reluctantly. "I planted a device in the bag, so I would be able to follow the kidnappers at a safe distance. They outsmarted me with that window trick. They would have been well outside the range of the signal by the time I got out to my car."

Her eyes narrowed.

"Ingenious. But why did it make that noise just now?"

"Because the bag is close by, Mrs Drummond," I said softly. "It's somewhere in this house."

She looked disdainful.

"But that's ridiculous."

"No, it isn't. It's like your daughter said. The machine has no brain. It doesn't reason. It just reports the facts. I have a theory about it. If I'm right, I'll be able to tell you why Napoleon Scotsman the Fourth was shot."

Clasping her hands together, she stared at her feet.

"I shall be very interested to hear that."

I scooped up the box from the floor.

"Mind if we go into the next room?"

I pointed inside. Angela shrugged, and we went through.

"You didn't tell me your mother had this house designed to match up with houses in her favorite movies."

She looked at me mystified.

"Scarcely important enough to mention, was it?"

"No," I admitted, "maybe not. Or you could take the other view. You could say it was important not to mention it."

"You'll have to explain that."

"I intend to." I pointed to the fireplace, where Napoleon Scotsman the Fourth had been stretched out on my first visit. "One of your mother's pictures was called 'Still Waters House'."

"Oh, that's one of my very favorites."

199

I wheeled around at the sound of the new voice. Joanna Towers stood there, a crumpled tea-towel in her hands. She beamed at me, and I waited for Angela to order her out. Instead, she said,

"Go on, Mr Preston."

"It must have been one of your mother's favorites too, Joanna. A lot of the inside of this house is a replica of Still Waters House. That fireplace now, that's exactly the same, to look at. I'm wondering whether it's just as phoney."

"Phoney?" squeaked Joanna, indignantly. "Do you mean imitation? Well, let me tell you, when it's really cold we have great log fires in that fireplace. A beautiful sight. You tell him, Angie."

Angie said, and I was surprised at the sudden kindness in her tone,

"Just be quiet a minute dear, there's a good girl. It's rude to interrupt. Mr Preston hasn't finished yet. Have you?"

"No," I agreed. "In the film, the house was being used, during the war between the States, as a hideout for Southern sympathisers. Nobody would ever find them, because of the fireplace. There was a secret room behind it. To get in, you had to pull out one of the carved figures at the side of the mantel.

One of these."

I yanked at a wooden owl. Nothing happened. The third figure along was a bald eagle. When I grabbed his head, he began to move. So did the fireplace. Smoothly, and on well-oiled hinges, it began to swing round in a circle.

'Angie. Look what he's doing, Angie."

Nobody took any notice of Joanna. I stared into the gloom behind the fireplace, but the sunlight couldn't reach very far inside. There were no gasps of astonishment from the Towers girls, and neither of them came forward to take a look. They didn't need to. And they were both behind me.

Where the hell was Thompson?

Angela's voice was very matter-of-fact.

"Well, now that you've satisfied your curiosity, perhaps you'd be good enough to put the room straight again."

She was one of the coolest people I ever met.

"Don't you want to look inside?" I queried.

"There's no need. It's just an empty space. We used to play in there, as girls." -

"No need?" I repeated.

Reaching down, I switched on my little box. It all but jumped off the floor in its excitement. I looked at Angela.

"I think there's a need," I told her. "Do you have a flashlight?"

"There's one on the wall inside," said Joanna brightly.

Her sister gave her a dirty look.

"Now, don't get cross with me, Angie. Mr Preston is going to have to go in there. You know that. There's no other way."

Angela seemed to give up some internal struggle. She put a tired hand to her face, and said in a resigned voice.

"No, I suppose not. Go ahead, Mr Preston."

But I had no intention of going into that darkness alone.

"After you, ladies."

"No. We're not coming," Angela refused.

"Oh yes you are, lady," I began.

The tea towel fluttered from Joanna's hands to the floor. It was my own fault, I cursed. I should never have left that Webley on the desk in the next room.

"Look what I found," twittered Joanna.

It was all so unreal. There was no threat in the voice, or the attitude. She could have been asking whether I'd stay to tea. The only threat came from that cold, staring metal in her hands.

I hoped the fear was all inside me, and not running down my forehead.

"I don't understand," I said, trying to sound calm. "Are you threatening me, Joanna?"

By way of reply, she stamped her foot in petulance.

"Oh dear, I hate this part. You know how I hate this, Angie."

Not as much as me, lady. But I said nothing, watching Angela. She stared at me for long seconds, then shook her head very slowly.

"Don't pretend to be so naive, Mr Preston. You knew, as well as I did, that something would have to happen, the moment you brought that confounded contraption in here. And for God's sake, turn it off."

I did that, and we all faced each other in silence.

"The whole thing was a set-up from the beginning," I said finally. "You planned it all to rob that nice old man. Your very dear friend."

Angela flinched at the sourness in my voice.

"I hated doing that. But there was no other way. I was desperate for money. The expense of all this—"

"And Uncle Tommy's kidnap—" I began. Joanna squawked in alarm.

"Oh Lordie, has somebody kidnapped poor Uncle Tommy? You never told me that, Angela. Why do you keep things from me? Oh my, whatever shall we do?"

"Be quiet, you fool. Uncle Tommy is fine. He's in his room, sleeping it off, as usual."

"Then why did Mr Preston say he was kidnapped?" demanded Joanna.

"I was going to say that he was never kidnapped at all," I assured her. "It's my guess that Angela locked him behind the fireplace, with a case of booze to keep him quiet. Nobody would ever look there, because no one knew about it. Except you two. That's right isn't it, Mrs Drummond?"

She shrugged.

"I've had to do it before, many times. To be certain that no one sees him, in that—that condition. He doesn't suffer."

"Then he was luckier than Mr Small," I continued. "At least your uncle is still alive."

This brought more agitation from the gun-toting Joanna.

"Now, who is this Mr Small? I demand to know, at once. I am absolutely sick and tired of the way you keep me in the dark, Angie, and I won't stand it a moment longer."

Angela's face was strained.

"His name wasn't Small," she explained. "Mr Preston is talking about that man Ross."

It was creepy, the way she kept referring to me as 'Mr', while leading up either to killing me, or sealing me up in that room.

Joanna pouted.

"Oh him. A nasty man. Really quite horrid. He actually threatened us. Did Angela tell you? Oh, I didn't mind about him at all."

I thought I could see a way out.

"But not me, Joanna. You don't dislike me. I'm nice. You made me some coffee the other day. Remember?"

She smiled, nodding.

"Of course I remember. A nice, friendly man. I told Angie, didn't I, Angie?"

Well, I like you too, Joanna. You wouldn't want to hurt me, now would you?"

"Oh no." She looked horrified at the thought. "Angie, we're not going to have to hurt him, are we?"

But Angela was ready for it.

"Of course not, dear. I wouldn't ask you to hurt anyone nice. But remember, I explained it to you before. If you keep on shooting, very quickly, Mr Preston won't feel any pain at all."

"Oh yes, of course." Joanna looked relieved, and turned back to me. "There you are, you see?"

I saw only too well. Except that I didn't understand what made any of it necessary in the first place.

"Tell me one thing, Mrs Drummond. I understand about your not wanting to part with the house, and all that. I can understand that you may have needed money badly. But enough is enough. I can't believe that you've done all this just to keep the house. Especially murder. No house justifies that. Why didn't you just admit you were licked, and sell the place?"

Angela Drummond drew herself up very straight. I had the feeling this was going to be it.

"None of us can ever leave here. None of us. And now, I'm sorry, but that has to include you. Joanna."

Joanna bit her lip.

"You mean now?"

"This instant."

My executioner nodded, and the gun came up level.

"Just what is going on here? Put that gun down, lady."

Sam Thompson's voice boomed behind the

two women. Joanna squawked in panic. I dived the six feet grabbing for the gun. There was a loud noise and a scream of pain. Then I was lying on the floor, the gun in my hand. Joanna was staring down at me in terror. Next to me on the carpet, Angela Drummond was clutching at her thigh, where dark blood welled slowly outwards.

"You took your time," I snapped at Thompson.

"Listen, there was this road accident."

"Never mind. Get cars, get ambulances, get everybody."

I went behind the fireplace, looking for the flashlight.

AFTERMATH

I lit my millionth cigarette and stared tiredly at the gray walls.

It was two in the morning, and I wanted to go home to bed. So did the Assistant District Attorney, by the look of him.

"Now then, let's just go over this."

He waved sheets of paper at me.

"We've been over it," I objected.

"So we'll go over it again. I'm a slow learner."

The close-cropped hair seemed to bristle as he glowered at me from hostile, suspicious eyes.

"Tell me what happened when you went in the cupboard."

"It wasn't a cupboard. It was a room," I corrected him. "It was bigger than this, for example. You want to call your office a cupboard?"

"Keep my office out of this. What happened in there?"

"First, I found the flashlight. It had a fresh battery, that was point one. Then I noticed how clean the place was. I'd been expecting an inch of dust, but there wasn't any. In the far corner was a narrow bed, and a chair. On the bed was the suitcase."

"With the money inside?"

"Right."

"Did you check it?"

I gave him my pained expression.

"Ever try checking that much money? It takes hours. No, I didn't. I lifted up the lid, and that's all. It seemed to be all there."

"You didn't slip a few bills in your pocket, for expenses?"

"If you'd care to say that again, when we're

away from this building, you'll get an answer."

He clucked in annoyance.

"Well, go on. What else?"

"I looked under the bed. Just habit. I could see the wall was damaged, so I pulled the bed clear. A hole had been knocked in the wall, with the bricks just put in place on top of each other. I took out the bricks to find out why. There was a skeleton in there."

"Male or female?" he demanded.

I looked to the ceiling for help. The ceiling stared back.

"You're not too well up on skeletons, are you?" I said nastily. "It takes a medical man to put a sex to one. Oh, and one arm seemed to be missing."

"But there was some clothing in there, a man's clothing?"

"Yes. There was a wallet in one pocket. It had a driving license in the name Augustus Drummond, one or two other papers."

"And what did you do then?"

"There was nothing for me to do. I went back out and waited for the police. My partner had already sent for them."

He read quickly, turning over a page.

"What did you think, about finding this Drummond's body?"

"I didn't find a body. It was a skeleton. And we weren't introduced," I reminded him. "What I think is not evidence."

The ADA waved in impatience.

"But you're not a complete fool," he snorted. "Plus, you've been closer to the family this past few days than anyone else has been in twenty years. Try a little speculation."

I leaned back, covering a yawn.

"Well, so long as we understand that's what it is. I think it was Angela's husband. I think he never left her at all, the way her sister tells it. And he didn't die away from home. Something went wrong between them, and Augustus got himself bumped off."

"You think Mrs Drummond killed him?"

"I'm not so sure. When it came time to bump me off, it was Joanna got the job. Frankly, with Angela being such a cool customer, and Joanna being just a little forgetful, I think you are going to have one helluva job proving just who did what to who."

"Whom," he corrected, absently. "It won't matter much, I fancy. They must have been in it together, after it happened. The question of who fired the shot becomes a little academic, after all these years. Did you work

210

out why the dog was killed?"

It was a complete switch. I blinked while adjusting.

"I thought I did, when I went to the house. The fireplace was a replica of the one in the movie, like I told you earlier. In the film, the secret room was given away by a dog. He jumped up and yanked on the lever with his teeth. I had half an idea that the Corgi might have repeated the trick, and put them in danger."

He'd had a lot of practise at looking disbelieving.

"Kind of far-fetched, wasn't it?"

"Well," I confessed lamely, "maybe I wasn't thinking too well. You got a better theory?"

He smirked with self-satisfaction.

"More than a theory. We have a fact. You recall the skeleton was missing an arm?"

"Yup."

"We found it. There was fresh earth just outside the house. When we turned it over, up came the arm. There were marks of a dog's teeth on it."

I shuddered.

"So old Napoleon had found the bones, and thought it was playtime?"

"Something of the kind. It must have been

211

while they were getting the room ready for old Mr Towers to be locked up. When you've managed to keep a murder secret all those years, you can't have it all upset by a dog, family friend or no."

It made about as much sense as anything else in that bizarre household.

"I never did get to meet the old man. How did you find him?"

"Drunk as a skunk. He'll be no use on the stand."

That was what I'd expected.

"And the dead man, Ross. Did you get a make on him yet?"

He nodded.

"An unsuccessful actor. This was his first time out as a crook."

"Another short career for him. Well, you'll be able to pin that on one of the sisters."

"We'll certainly try."

I held up my watch-arm.

"I don't want to seem uncooperative and all, but do you ever get sleep on this job?"

He affected surprise.

"Good heavens, is that the time? Let's all go home. Take a break from this. Can you be here in the morning? Say eight o'clock?"

"I can be here in the morning, say ten o'clock."

About to give me an argument, he changed his mind.

"Ten, then. Sharp."

I went back to Parkside. There was a note pushed through the door. It was from the Isobel Towers Appreciation Society, and told me in curt terms that because of the unfavourable publicity I'd brought to the family—that's what it said—my membership would be terminated. It was signed by Alexander Cilento.

At the foot was a hand-written addition. It said that if I was interested in re-admission, I should call. That part was signed 'Claire'.

I grinned, tired as I was.

Re-admission.

Well, we'd see.

The publishers hope that this book has given you enjoyable reading. Large Print Books are especially designed to be as easy to see and hold as possible. If you wish a complete list of our books, please ask at your local library or write directly to: Magna Print Books, Long Preston, North Yorkshire, BD23 4ND England.